THE NIGHT COMETH
20 FANTASTICAL SHORT STORIES

LORILYN ROBERTS

REAR GUARD PUBLISHING, INC.

DEDICATION

For Anne Franczek

CONTENTS

1

THE EMPTY PAPER TRAY

John 3:16 (NKJV)

For God so loved the world that He gave His only
begotten Son, that whoever believes in Him
should not perish but have everlasting life.

As a former court reporter, I spent twenty years reporting depositions, court hearings, and legal proceedings. I would imagine today's courtroom etiquette is very much the same. A jury is seated. The plaintiff presents his case, and then the defendant gives his evidence to refute the plaintiff's claims. Frequently, supporting documents will be introduced as exhibits. Of course, the judge has the final authority over the proceedings and the evidence entered into the record.

———

One night I had an encounter of a different kind. I stood alone in a courtroom before a judge seated behind a high bench. No jury was present to hear the evidence, no witnesses would be called, and no exhibits marked. A lawyer did not represent me.

I pondered my very unceremonious fate. Unceremonious because no one was with me—no family, friends, witnesses, or reporters.

As I awaited sentencing, something strange happened. My stenograph machine began to spit out reams of paper at a speed that wasn't humanly possible.

While I couldn't read the words on the paper, I knew what those markings represented. A record of my life was on full display to be examined by the judge. The notes continued to unravel and overflow from the tray faster and faster until thousands of interconnected loops of stenograph paper entombed my body.

I knew I was guilty of innumerable crimes. I had never killed someone, robbed a bank, or committed an act that would send me to jail; at least not by human standards. But God's moral code is different. He demands perfection, and I had not lived a perfect life. One tiny wrongdoing would condemn me to hell. I knew I had committed many unrighteous acts, not just one.

I longed to fix my mistakes, but I couldn't. It was too late, and I had no defense. As the judge was about to sentence me, a lone figure came forward. The man towered over me, and I was overwhelmed by his appearance. Dare I look into his eyes? The room was empty except for the three of us, and then, unexpectedly, God revealed himself. I recognized the figure as Jesus.

Jesus had chosen to stand beside me in my darkest hour. Only he could make a difference. Only he could change the course of my future. No money, politician, lawyer, pastor, or friend could save me. Jesus came to my rescue in the hour of my greatest need. I prayed the judge would listen to him.

My mediator approached the bench, and a private conversation ensued outside my hearing. The spectacle of my life was no secret to the judge or Jesus. Every sin I had ever committed, every secret thought, every wasted action, every omission, and every commission of something wrong was laid bare.

As I grappled with my sin, I knew my destiny. Unless my mediator intervened, I would spend eternity in hell.

Suddenly, the reams of stenograph paper covering my body flipped over and backward and recoiled back inside the tray. I saw the words on the paper disappear. The scroll of my life was "remembered no more." No record could be made or court reporter's notes transcribed.

Stunned, I turned my focus to the bench conference. Jesus stepped down and stood beside me. Without warning, the reams of paper began to unravel once more, and this time the steno paper of my sinful life wrapped around my redeemer. Then the bailiff appeared and took Jesus away in handcuffs.

———

The gravity of what Jesus did two thousand years ago on the cross is unfathomable. Not only did Jesus die for me, but he died for you. He died for every human being who has ever lived.

The short stories in this book grapple with many prophetic events that Jesus warned about, and most stories are about supernatural encounters.

In these last days, we will see more unexplainable events unfolding than at any other time in history. I pray the reader will think deeply about these things.

Most people do not see the signs of Jesus' return, but they are everywhere. Do not be deceived by the devil's wiles. The hour is late. Let us not grow weary in serving our Savior because Jesus is returning soon.

2

SEDUCING SPIRITS

1 Timothy 6:6 (NKJV)

Now godliness with contentment is great gain.

Braylon had it all. At thirty-three, he had climbed the ladder of corporate success like no other. By the end of the year, he hoped to be vice president of manufacturing of a Fortune 500 company.

Not only was he rich, but his wife's good looks made his friends envious. His daughter was the youngest member of the city orchestra playing lead violin, and his dogs were champions in every sense of the word. Their house had six bathrooms, and he drove a Tesla Model X. What more was there for him to achieve?

Despite all that success, Braylon knew something was missing. He checked his horoscope faithfully each morning as he ate his oatmeal breakfast, but the prognostication was always vague, leading to more than one meaning or interpretation.

On this sunny morning, he finished his second cup of coffee in the bathroom, brushed his teeth, and combed his hair. As he checked his appearance in the mirror, one gray hair appeared. He covered it up with some strands of dark brown hair and vowed to get his hair colored as soon as possible.

Braylon grabbed his briefcase near the stairs, exited through the garage door, and hopped into his electric car. After fighting through heavy traffic for twenty minutes, he arrived five minutes late. He scolded himself; he shouldn't have had that second cup of coffee. Now he would have to rush through City Square to make it on time. Why did anyone set a mandatory meeting before nine?

In City Square, a short distance from his car, a street preacher shouted through a bullhorn, "Repent, for the kingdom of God is near."

"What an idiot," Braylon mumbled under his breath. Several homeless men listened attentively nearby, and another hopeless bum handed out pamphlets.

Braylon mocked them as he passed. "Go get a job; do something with your life."

Eyes stared at Braylon, but nobody said anything.

Disgusted, Braylon kept walking. Farther up the sidewalk, just past City Square, he noticed a small business with a red neon sign flashing *Palmistry & Fortune-Telling. No Appointment Necessary.* Several people stood outside waiting to enter.

Braylon had walked this way hundreds of times on his way to and from work, but today the colorful advertisement caught his attention. So many people were inside—what did they know that he didn't? Palmistry & Fortune-Telling was doing a very brisk business.

Could a fortune-teller read his palm and tell him if he would reach the pinnacle of corporate success? He made a mental note to check out the opportunity later.

The day flew by, perhaps because one issue after another needed Braylon's attention. By the time five rolled around, he was exhausted. However, the gnawing discontentment was more than his usual tiredness. He had an excellent job, tons of money, an immaculate reputation—which couldn't be said about most people he knew—and a lovely wife and daughter. But none of those things filled that empty place in his heart.

His thoughts returned to Palmistry & Fortune-Telling. He glanced at the clock. If he left now, he could stop by before they closed. He locked his office and said a quick goodbye to several still working. He didn't feel guilty leaving—he had worked plenty of late-night hours to achieve his position. And once he set his mind on something, nothing could deter him. At the very least, a personal visit with a fortune-teller would be better than the vague horoscope he read each morning.

As Braylon entertained these thoughts, he remembered his hero, Alexander the Great. By the time Alexander was 33, he had conquered all the known world. A driven man, Alexander continued his exploits until his generals rebelled and said, "No more." And then he suddenly died.

Braylon shook his head. What a horrible end to a remarkable career. Just thinking about Alexander's demise at such a young age greatly disturbed Braylon. He rode the elevator down to the lobby and hurried out the door. Checking his watch, he hustled toward City Square. What time did the business close?

The red neon sign was still flashing as he neared Palmistry & Fortune-Telling. Braylon relaxed, slowing his pace. They must not close until six. He adjusted his tie and ran his fingers through his hair. Once he arrived and felt presentable, he opened the door. The fragrance of burning incense filled his nostrils. Across the room, an older man in tattered clothes sat on a wooden chair with his eyes closed. The palm reader appeared to be in deep meditation. Soft music hummed in the background, and multi-colored crystal rocks surrounded the indoor waterfall.

Braylon wasn't sure what to do. Surely the man heard him enter. As Braylon was about to speak, the store owner opened his eyes.

"I knew you would come today," he said.

"You knew I would come?" Braylon repeated.

The man nodded. "I'm Davu. What can I do for you?"

Braylon hesitated. Shouldn't the fortune-teller know why he came? But before Braylon could say anything, the Seer continued. "I see you pass by here every day, always in a hurry."

Braylon nodded. "Yes, I'm a busy executive." He cleared his throat. What do you tell a fortune-teller? If wisdom were measurable in human years, Braylon surmised Davu would be very wise. He certainly looked like he had been around a long time.

"I have everything any man could want, but—I'm not happy," he confessed. "I'm searching for something, and I don't know what it is."

"Come near me," the fortune-teller said.

Braylon hesitated. Was he ready to take the next step? "How much does a palm reading cost?"

Davu replied, "The first reading is always free."

Braylon thought about it. If he wasn't going to charge him, he wouldn't be out any money if the worst thing happened. He bit his lip. "If I don't have to make a long-term commitment"—he glanced at his watch—"how long will it take?"

The Seer walked over to the counter. "Just fill out this form. I have a room in the back where I'll do the reading. As I said, there's no charge for the first one."

Braylon thought that made good business sense. "Let's do it."

After completing the personal history/information sheet, Davu directed him to the reading room.

"I'll be back in a couple of minutes. I want to lock up the business, as you are my last client for the day, and turn off the computer. That way, we won't have any interruptions. Please, make yourself comfortable."

Braylon did as the fortune-teller directed, and a few minutes later, Davu reappeared. He sat beside Braylon with a table between them. "Place one of your hands here."

Braylon put his right hand on the table, and then Davu waved a magnifying glass over his palm under a very bright light. Braylon watched as he analyzed the creases and the lines. Whatever there was to see, Braylon was intrigued; how could the fortune-teller reveal anything about Braylon's life just by reading his palm?

After a few minutes, Davu set down his magnifying glass and locked eyes with Braylon. "You'll never be content. Nothing can make you happy."

Braylon couldn't believe his ears. He came here and wasted half an hour to have some stupid fortune-teller tell him nothing would make him happy. Now he was angry.

Thankful he hadn't wasted any money, he stood. "I see, Seer, that you don't see. I will be on my way now."

Davu showed him to the door as Braylon did his best to control his emotions. Once again, the fortune-teller repeated the utterance, "You'll never be content," and added, "Only death will bring you contentment."

Braylon remembered his hero, Alexander the Great, and thought he would lose his temper if the Seer said that one more time. He rushed out the door, and only when he was far away did he allow himself to relax.

Now he felt foolish. What was the big deal? He slowed his walk but heard a voice inside his head, "You've been cursed."

Braylon tried to dismiss it, but he swore he heard those words—perhaps not audibly, but loudly enough to know what was said. As he pondered how that was possible, he sensed somebody following him. He glanced back, but no one was there.

He broke out in a cold sweat and hurried back to his car. As he passed City Square, he noticed the Jesus freaks weren't there. They must have left early. He quickly found his vehicle and slid into the driver's seat, relieved to be safe, even if it was just glass and metal surrounding him.

He let the electric car drive itself home—there were some perks to being rich. Suddenly, he couldn't resist checking the back seat.

"Blast that Seer," he mumbled. Not only was he not content—he was terrified. Suppose he was cursed, as the voice said?

———

Three Days Later

The feeling that someone was following Braylon wouldn't leave. "Maybe I should see a shrink," he muttered as he pulled into the parking lot earlier than usual. He needed to get this all figured out. Some steep competition faced him for the title of vice president of manufacturing, and the multi-million dollar company wouldn't want a psycho on their board.

Once again, he passed the street preacher and the pamphlet thumper. The same man was still shouting the same message, "Repent, for the kingdom of God is near."

Braylon brushed past him as another man tried to hand him a pamphlet. Braylon shoved his hand away. "Not interested," and continued at a good clip down the street. As he neared Palmistry & Fortune-Telling, he took a wide detour. Just seeing the flashing sign made him uncomfortable. No sooner had he done so, however, when he perceived somebody following him.

Braylon looked behind him. To his surprise, this time, he saw someone. Braylon presumed he was a man. He wore a dark robe with a shawl-like head covering, but he was too far back to make out his facial features.

Visibly shaken, Braylon started running away from the ghost-like figure. After a reasonable distance, he glanced back but no longer saw anyone.

"Good riddance," Braylon said, and he continued walking, even indulging in some fanciful thoughts. How nice that paycheck would be if he earned the title of vice president. Now he hoped to achieve it if for no reason than to prove the Seer wrong. That phony guy didn't know anything.

The day quickly passed, and at closing time, Braylon became fearful—again. He could immerse himself in business activities all day, but panic and fear would overtake his persona when he left the office in the evening. He hated that he had to pass by the fortune-teller's business. Even with a wide detour, he imagined the Seer watching him.

Tonight, he decided to try something different. He would enter another business he usually passed by and see if anyone appeared. Then he could prove to himself that it was all his imagination.

"I have a date with my wife," he told his secretary. She smiled as he skirted by her on his way to the door.

Once outside, he looked in each direction at least three times. Seeing no one, he proceeded. No sooner had he gone a short distance, however, when he felt the person in the dark robe following him. He didn't need to look. It had happened every day since he visited the palm reader.

Braylon found a partially hidden doorway where he would wait, and once the stalker passed, he would step out and ask, "Why are you following me?"

Braylon wanted to get this nightmare over with so he could get on with his life—content or not. His heart thumped so loudly he feared it would give away his presence. Sweat beaded on his brow.

Braylon heard the stalker approaching, but he didn't come nearer. "He must know where I'm hiding," Braylon mused. "I will just have to confront him."

No sooner had Braylon determined to do that when the stalker appeared in front of him. Braylon saw his face for the first time, and his features horrified him. Terror gripped his heart, and he almost vomited on the sidewalk.

"Who are you?" Braylon asked.

"I am Death," the man said.

Braylon tried to back away, but the alley hemmed him in, and there was no place to go. How could he get around the demon? "Why are you following me? Go away."

"I can take you to a place where you'll be content forever. Isn't that what you want?"

Braylon shoved the man out of the way and took off toward City Square. He cursed the palm reader as he ran by the building. Out of breath and faint with terror, he came to the bullhorn blaster and the pamphlet thumper—and cursed them, too.

Then he gathered enough strength to run to his car and jumped inside. Trembling, he sat for a moment to catch his breath. How could he put this nightmare out of his mind?

He started his car and had finished backing out of his reserved parking spot when he felt, again, someone watching him. "Get a hold of yourself," Braylon muttered, "or you'll go crazy."

He put his transmission in the forward position, and when he looked in his rearview mirror, much to his horror, he saw Death. His foot froze on the gas pedal. The last thing Braylon remembered was water spraying from the fire hydrant over the front of his wrecked car.

"I'm dead," he muttered.

———

Braylon woke up in the hospital with his wife and daughter by his bedside. When he looked into their fearful eyes, for the first time in a long time, he saw something unexpected—love. Feeling groggy, he wanted to be sure he was alive and not dead.

His wife leaned over and kissed him. "I'm glad you woke up," she said. "I love you so much."

Tears came to Braylon's eyes. "I love you, too, Honey. I'm sorry."

His daughter crowded by his bed. "Love you, Dad."

"How did I get here?" Braylon asked.

His wife turned away briefly. She seemed to be speaking to somebody in the hallway.

Then she turned her focus back to Braylon, "I want you to meet Jess and John. They saw you crash into the fire hydrant, called an ambulance, and then rushed over to see if you needed help. They used their shirts as a tourniquet to stop the bleeding. Your blood pressure was so low; that's why they admitted you."

His wife and daughter cleared out of the way. To his surprise, the street preacher and pamphlet thumper stood before him. "You saved my life?" he asked.

Jess, who had tried numerous times to hand him a pamphlet, smiled. "You passed by us every day. We knew you needed Jesus, so we prayed for an opportunity to witness to you."

John, the preacher with the bullhorn, nodded. "Only through Jesus can you find hope. God saved your life. Death was knocking at the door, but God preserved your life."

"Can God bring me contentment?" Braylon asked.

His daughter stepped forward. "I found Jesus, and he has given me joy."

"How?" Braylon asked. "Somebody cursed me, and now Death is trying to kill me. He was even in the car with me," and then Braylon realized how stupid he sounded. "Must be the medicine they gave me. It's making me say crazy things."

"May we pray with you to receive Jesus?" John asked.

Braylon had never heard those words. "What do I have to do?"

"Believe that Jesus died for your sins, repent, and live each day for him. Then you will find contentment in this world and hope for the world to come."

"That's it?" Braylon asked.

"That's it," Jess said as he handed Braylon the pamphlet he had rejected many times.

This time, however, Braylon took it. With tears in his eyes, he prayed, "Forgive me, Jesus."

3

MIRROR, MIRROR

Colossians 3:23-24 (NKJV)

And whatever you do, do it heartily, as to the Lord
and not to men, knowing that from the Lord you
will receive the reward of the inheritance; for you
serve the Lord Christ.

D r. William Christiansen pulled up to the beach house with his wife and two daughters.

"We're here," he exclaimed. He turned off the engine and pointed. "And the house is right on the ocean."

His teenage daughters squealed.

"Go check it out. Your mom and I will join you later."

The girls leaped out of the car.

William winked at his wife. "That didn't take too much convincing."

She surveyed the sandy shoreline and choppy waves in the distance. "It's a dream come true; one week away from everything."

William nodded. "With my brother and his family."

William was a highly successful doctor with a thriving medical practice. He had been nominated for a significant award for his work on pancreatic cancer and even recently appeared on Fox News, Bloomberg, and CNN.

As those thoughts swirled in the doctor's head, he thought about the attention he had received from strangers. However, the toll on his family was steep. With all the deadlines, presentations, expectations, and media hype behind his promising cure, he wasn't sure it was worth it.

In contrast, his brother, Noah, had done much for the kingdom of God. Why couldn't he be like his brother—faithful to God and the truth?

But, for now, William was thankful to be with his family. He hoped this vacation would help him to get back on track.

He stepped out of the car, and his phone chirped. "Almost there."

William smiled. "Noah will be here in a few minutes. Why don't you make sure the house meets your expectations, and I'll stay here and wait for him."

His wife adjusted the sun hat over her eyes. "In this heat?"

William nodded. "You go. I'll be there soon."

Before heading to the vacation beach house, his wife stepped back into the car and grabbed a few things.

As she disappeared, William reminisced how he loved his wife now more than the day he married her. When had he last thanked God for his family?

———

Pastor Noah Christensen exclaimed, "We're almost there," as if the rest of his family hadn't figured it out.

The two teen boys cheered in the back of the van.

When the family pulled into the driveway, Noah saw his brother leaning against the car, waiting for him.

Noah's wife smiled. "You and your famous brother have much catching up to do."

Noah squirmed. His twin brother was a successful doctor, but she didn't need to rub it in. While William was winning international awards, Noah was pastoring a small church of two hundred members. However, recently, the church no longer felt like a bastion for the weary and the hopeless. Members had become preoccupied with social justice, wokeness, and inclusivity. Many of the congregants wanted to get rid of him.

Elders had met two weeks earlier to discuss firing him. A new controversy erupted every week. Discouraged, he wanted to walk away from it all. Perhaps they were right; his suffering was because of his unwillingness to compromise.

Even though he hadn't told anyone, Noah planned on turning in his resignation. He believed his ministry had failed despite many coming to a saving knowledge of Jesus Christ.

The boys quickly exited the car and headed for the beach.

His wife put on her sunglasses. "I'll leave you to catch up with your brother." Her eyes followed the steps to the beach house. "I can't wait to see the inside."

Noah nodded. In his heart, though, her words pricked him. A whole week to feel inferior to his brother. He didn't begrudge what his brilliant brother had accomplished. He only wished he could have had the same success as a pastor.

William hurried over to greet Noah as he stepped out of the car. "Hey, Brother."

The twins embraced. "It's been too long," William said. "And your boys have grown so much."

Noah smiled. "Where are your girls?"

William glanced toward the beach. "They took off that way."

Noah chuckled. "Our kids will find each other."

In many ways, the twin brothers' lives paralleled each other. Except William had become a doctor, and Noah had become a pastor. William was wealthy and respected in the medical community. Noah was disrespected and hated by many in his church. William had a bright future. Noah couldn't bear to think about his.

But for now, Noah would be thankful for this time with his brother, William. He wouldn't tell his brother that his church wanted to fire him. Resigning sounded better than being fired.

———

William clutched his brother on the shoulder. "Let's go for a walk, shall we?"

Noah looked at his shoes.

As if William could read his twin brother's mind, he chirped, "Leave them in the car. Come on, before we get busy with family stuff. Let's go."

Noah didn't need much convincing. He flipped off his shoes, and they made a beeline to the beach.

William remembered their summer vacations as kids when they would kick beach balls, build sandcastles, and look for sand crabs. Those memories were sweet to William, but they seemed like eons ago. He longed for that time again when he didn't feel burdened with so much responsibility. He felt like he was sinking under the expectations of an overreaching medical complex. "Publish, publish, publish," his superiors would say, "so we can get more funding."

William only wanted his brother to tell him inspiring stories about God's blessings. He tried to imagine how awesome it would be to serve a God-fearing congregation and an elder board that loved the Lord. William couldn't remember the last time his family had attended church regularly. He was out of town so much—and while he longed for church fellowship, he could never find the time to make it happen.

"How is your church?" William asked. "Are you growing? Many new converts? How about those missionaries in Africa? Do they need more money?"

That was always William's answer for not attending church regularly. Send more money. Not that money wasn't necessary for missions, but—was there more God wanted from him?

Noah evaded answering for a minute to couch his words positively. "The church is going through some tough times."

William nodded as he stopped to soak his feet in a freshly made water hole. "Yeah, I suppose with all this woke stuff and gender confusion and social justice"—he paused for a second. "Of course, I'd rather deal with that than—"

"Than what?" Noah asked.

"Ah, just all the political stuff. Practicing medicine is harder when the government tells you what you can and can't do, what you can and can't prescribe, you know, all that stuff you hear in the news."

Noah quipped. "But everyone respects you, William. You practically run the medical research at the University. Without you, their funding would disappear."

William shook his head. "Everybody owns me. Sometimes I feel like a pawn in a chess match waiting to be wiped off the board for some idiotic king who thinks he's God. At least in church, you are surrounded by people who seek the truth and want to improve the world. With you as their pastor, the church should be thankful. You'd never compromise God's word for—for popularity."

———

Noah couldn't state the truth. His unwillingness to compromise had cost him the pastorate. If his brother knew the truth, if he really knew—suddenly, a crazy thought swirled in his head. What if they traded places for a few days? He would be William, and William would be him. They would only let their family in on the hoax. Being twins, no one would know the difference. All their lives, people had confused them, even those who knew them well. But before suggesting it, his brother blurted out exactly what he was thinking.

"Let's trade places," William said. "You be me for a couple of days."

Noah pretended not to want to go along with it.

"Noah," William said. "I need a diversion. I haven't been to church in so long. I'd give anything to be around God-fearing church-goers. I don't want this fame and notoriety. It's not what everybody thinks it is."

Noah couldn't believe his ears. Could they pull this off? Maybe

God had planned all of this out and brought them to the beach for a week to make it happen.

Besides, Noah imagined William's battles being easy compared to his. William had no idea what it was like to pastor a church where the people hated you. And to be admired by doctors, the media, and the University—how could that be hard to handle? Of course, he didn't know a thing about medicine. He certainly couldn't practice it, or he would go to jail. But he could sit in his brother's office, wear a white coat, and feel important.

"Okay. I'm all in," Noah said. "Not for very long, though, or we could get into trouble. If we did get caught, we'd call it a joke. Nobody needs to know except our family."

The brothers continued talking about how they could pull off the hoax. As they talked, the plan grew, taking on a life of its own.

Suddenly, the cries of someone in the ocean reached their ears.

"A waterspout," Noah exclaimed. "My God, somebody is caught in it."

The brothers ran toward the water—was it one of their children?

At last, they could see the person struggling in the water. Thank God he was alive, although he was in trouble. Noah followed William into the swirling waves. The victim was an older man, perhaps in his sixties. The brothers struggled through the cresting tide as the spout tossed water everywhere. The undertow was stronger than Noah had ever felt. If he weren't trying to save the dying man, he would have been terrified that he would drown.

Noah prayed, "Please, Lord, help us."

With the man choking and gasping for air, the brothers managed to haul him to shore. The waterspout dissipated, and the sudden calmness of the water seemed supernatural. William laid the man gently on the sand. As a doctor, he knew what to do. And Noah, a Godly man, prayed like the man's life depended on it.

Together, the twin brothers worked on the rescued man. After a short time, the man revived and sat up. Noah praised God, "Thank you, Jesus. Thank you for answering our prayers."

Dr. Christensen continued to assess him. "We need to call an ambulance, or do you have a relative we can contact?"

The man peered into William's eyes with such intensity Noah saw fear on his brother's face. Was there more to this near drowning than Noah recognized?

As the brothers waited for the man to answer William's question, the man stood abruptly.

The brothers stared in amazement. How could he recover so quickly?

"Who are you?" Noah asked.

"Do not be afraid," the man said. "You wanted to save me. In doing so, you saved yourselves. He glanced at William. "You are a doctor," and then he looked at Noah. "And you are a pastor."

The two brothers exchanged glances. Who was this man? How could he know their profession? Noah knew his brother was thinking the same thing.

"The reality is," the man said, "I saved you from losing your rewards. Salvation is a gift, but rewards are earned. Think about it. Each of you wants what your twin brother has. Is that not like Satan, to fool you into believing that what the other person has is better?"

Speechless, Noah and William stared at the man.

"Don't believe the devil's lies. Do what God has called you to do. If it's suffering, suffer with joy. If it's success, give God the glory. If it's weariness, persevere. Accept your lot in life with humility. Love God when things are easy and when they aren't. If you do that, heavenly awards await you."

Several seconds passed until the brothers could speak, and the man disappeared.

"We just had a vision," Noah said.

William nodded. "The first thing I'm going to do is—repent."

Noah's pride evaporated. "Things have been terrible at my church."

William interrupted him. "That's because you stand for truth.

Don't compromise, Noah," William said. "You heard what the angel said."

The voices of four teens approaching interrupted their supernatural encounter. Noah said, "We need to pray for our children."

"I must spend more time with my family," William said. "I must. I've been warned."

"Giving up is not an option," Noah said. "I will never resign." He looked up into the heavens. "Today is the first day of the rest of my life. I feel like I've been born again."[1]

4

HAVE PINK SUITCASE - WILL TRAVEL

Proverbs 3:5-6 (NKJV)

Trust in the Lᴏʀᴅ with all your heart, and lean not on
your own understanding; in all your ways
acknowledge Him, and He shall direct your paths.

H ailey Becker was all of 79 years old. She lived with her doting, younger husband for the better part of her life, and they had two wonderful grown daughters who lived nearby. They were one of those families you couldn't help but like. Hailey was the best cook this side of paradise, and Charlie could be anybody's uncle—even the mothers-in-law who gossiped too much. Charlie knew how to be polite and caring, and a pot of coffee was always brewing whenever I stopped by.

So when we heard about an upcoming surprise trip, everybody

wanted to know the details. However, Charlie could keep a secret like no one, and Hailey—I'm not sure she knew all the details.

A few weeks later, Hailey called me. "You must come by and see my new suitcase," she said. "When we went to Cuba, our suitcases were too small for all the stuff we bought. We had to ship the vases back, and I worried for weeks when they didn't arrive."

I stopped in to see her bright pink new suitcase. What did her hubby think about the pink luggage? Knowing Charlie, he would say it was perfect.

"I wanted to be able to find my suitcase amongst the hundreds of others. You know, they all look the same when they pull them off the boat."

I once went on a cruise and came home with somebody else's luggage. And I didn't even notice it wasn't my bag until I opened it and found high heels stashed inside.

I laughed. "Sounds like a good strategy," although I couldn't imagine Hailey being like me and coming home with anybody else's suitcase.

Several months went by, and Hailey talked about the upcoming trip on several occasions. I heard through the grapevine that her suitcase was packed. One day she told me, "You know, I keep telling Charlie he needs to pack his bag. Mine is ready, but he hasn't even started packing his. We sure don't want to miss the boat. What can I do to get him to pack his clothes?"

"You know how men are," I said. "They can pack in three minutes."

Hailey's eyes twinkled. "Not me. I like to be ready at a moment's notice. Unexpected things can come up, and it would be dreadful to miss the boat because I packed too late."

I smiled. "Charlie won't let you down. He'll be at your side when you board that ship. I promise."

Soon signs revealed the trip was imminent. I heard that the suitcase was beside Hailey's bed, where she spent most of her days now. She was ready whenever the moment arrived.

Then I received word that they were going to the departure gate. Charlie reassured me he had her ticket in hand and her belongings were in the pink suitcase. He would make sure she was comfortable as she stood at the gate. I couldn't wait to say goodbye to my friend.

When I arrived, Hailey's bubbly personality enveloped me. She pointed to her bags, "I'm ready," she exclaimed, "but I still don't understand why Charlie hasn't packed very much." After a few minutes, she added, "I'm not going to worry about him. If he wants to wear the same clothes every day, that's his choice."

"He'll be fine," I assured my friend.

"When are we leaving?" Hailey asked Charlie several times as I sat beside her. "I don't want to miss the trip."

Charlie took her hand in his and locked onto her pleading eyes. "I promise you won't miss it."

I stopped by the departure gate several times until she made the trip to Glory. I heard her leaving was peaceful. And I also heard that she didn't need the suitcase she had meticulously packed.

I thought about everything I've packed away, not only in my house but in my heart. Then I remind myself it's an all-expense paid, one-way trip, and we don't need anything except our passport.

"She wasn't one minute late," Charlie reassured me, "and the smile on her face lifted my sorrowful heart."

Who greeted her when she arrived? I'm sure it was a glorious reunion of friends, family, and Bible heroes. When it's my turn, I know Hailey will be there to meet me.

Hailey Becker is not just my friend. She's everybody's friend. She is all those we've loved and said goodbye to too soon. And even though I know I won't need a suitcase, like Hailey, I want to be ready at a moment's notice. I find comfort in knowing my bag is packed—a bag filled by my Savior with love, joy, peace, patience, kindness, goodness, gentleness, faithfulness, and self-control. I must remember to refill it from God's holy book each day so I'm always ready should my name be called.

I imagine Hailey received so many gifts upon arrival that she was glad she didn't bring that earthly pink suitcase. While we try to fill our lives with worldly wealth, the wealth in Glory will far surpass anything we could conjure up here. Indeed, I suppose all the pink suitcases in the world could not contain the treasures awaiting us when we arrive.

I've also heard that I won't need a winter coat or any clothes. By all accounts, the weather is perfect, the land exquisite, the joy unspeakable, the citizens glorious, and the price exceptional—by that, I mean, it's free to pass holders—bought and paid for a long time ago by Jesus Christ. Every day I make sure I've packed my pass. The truth is, it's so big, heavy, and heavenly that no pink suitcase could ever contain it. And only Jesus Christ could carry it.[1]

5

RARER THAN THE GOLD OF OPHIR

Isaiah 13:12 (NKJV)

I will make a mortal more rare than fine gold, a man more than the golden wedge of Ophir.

"Why do you strike the fish above the eyes," Emma asked her dad.

Jace remembered what he said to his beautiful daughter those many years ago. "That's a good question, Emma. The reason is that you want to stun the fish into unconsciousness so when you bleed him out, he doesn't suffer."

"Oh," she said as she watched.

His wife edged over to Emma. "There's no need to traumatize her," and she redirected Emma's attention elsewhere.

Emma was only ten then, and it was her first fishing trip. Kate, his wife, had reluctantly agreed to go. She wasn't the outdoor type, but Jace, having no sons, hoped to instill the value of living off the land into his daughter before she grew up, and a lucky man stole her heart. Sometimes he would say to her when she was a teenager, "I hope your future husband loves hunting and fishing."

Kate was right. Jace had performed the bludgeoning act so often that he didn't even think about it. After throwing the unconscious fish into the ice cooler, the survivalist steered his new Stealth 210 aluminum crappie boat to the dock on Lake Istokpoga. After a successful day fishing, he remembered, before everything changed, how he looked forward to eating crappie for the next week. Nostalgia swept over him. That seemed so insignificant now.

As Emma grew up, Jace made sure she had a survivalist mentality. "You never know what the future holds," he would say. "Better be prepared for anything."

Kate, his wife, wasn't the least bit interested. She was only interested in the Bible regarding those topics. She would tell him, "I trust the Lord to take care of us," and Jace would reply, "The Lord helps those who help themselves."

What if Jace had known then what he knew now? What would he have said to her?

But Jace was a pragmatist. None of the religions in the world could put food on the table, and it didn't take a rocket scientist to see food shortages were coming. Grudgingly, Kate agreed to stock up on food and other necessities just in case the worst scenario unfolded. Still, Jace reasoned, as long as they had the 27,000-acre lake stocked with crappie, the family should never go without food.

In return, Kate asked Jace to go to church. Jace kept his part of the bargain for several years, but when the church started teaching about the rapture, he and Kate had a blow-up. "Nowhere in the Bible does the word 'rapture' appear," Jace said, and he quit attending.

While dismissing his wife's urgings to read the Bible and pray, Emma was different. "You need Jesus," she would say. "Suppose the rapture happens. You might have a lot of skills and be able to survive all seven years of the Tribulation, but you don't have to go through it if you believe Jesus died on the cross for your sins."

Jace had replayed those memory tapes in his head ad nauseum. Now he couldn't stop them. They ran on autoplay. His focus returned to the present as he reached his destination. The last time he was here, a small stream percolated through the sandy forest. Now it was just a barren wasteland hemmed in with dead, gray-bearded trees from lack of rain.

He sighed. He had spent the last three years in the Ocala National Forest after he lost his home because he couldn't pay the property taxes. "The water table must be near zero," he mused. The rains had been sparse for a year or more. Where could he go for water?

Depression sank into his soul. He was in this predicament because of the choices he had made. Now those conversations, a distant memory, tortured him. Jace trusted his skills as a survivalist with total disregard for the Bible.

The media and globalists blamed the disappearance of millions of people worldwide on aliens who came in UFOs and "beamed" them up. They said the aliens took all the troublemakers and left the best people behind.

Why did he listen to those liars? His wife and daughter weren't malcontents. He believed the news headlines for a long time, but eventually, he asked questions. Did that make sense? He had been duped, like an ostrich with his head in the sand.

Since Emma and Kate's disappearance, the hour hand of time swept faster as the days and nights decreased in length. While it bothered Jace not knowing what day, month, or year it was, the speeding up of time was the least of anyone's problems. People made it whatever day they wanted, just like they made up everything else.

Jace stared at the empty riverbed. Where had all the water gone? The dead trees made him sad because so many creatures had called the forest their home. Soon a sandy desert would reclaim the land.

It was so subtle and bizarre how it all began. Jace returned from work to an empty house one day, turned on the news, and heard the headlines.

"Do not panic," the religious guru said. "We've been tracking the skies with the VATT telescope at Mt. Graham, Arizona. Our observatory in Castel Gandolfo, Italy, is in contact with astronomers, and our sources have assured us everything is going as planned."

"What does that mean?" a reporter asked. "Millions have disappeared."

"We should know by tomorrow what the aliens' demands are, but we're confident their intentions are peaceful. They wanted to remove all the troublemakers on the planet to allow a more peaceful coexistence for those left behind."

The interview lasted a while, but Jace tuned it out. Were they really aliens? Where was the evidence? Or was this the rapture? Which story was more believable?

At first, Jace believed what the government said. The media seemed so sincere; after all, they had the facts, right? What did the aliens want?

Because of the speeding up of time, Jace began to mark on paper each night he slept, but there were so many Xs now he didn't bother to count them. However, if he had to guess, he would say it was eight years since the day millions disappeared.

As the pain of surviving intensified, memories of Emma and Kate became more dream-like, and every time he thought about them, he sunk into a tempestuous depression. Great effort and skill were the only ways to survive in a world without adequate food and water, and his gloominess made it more challenging.

Initially, life was relatively easy and calm after the disappearances, perhaps to give people time to grieve for their loved ones, but that didn't last long. Soon a reset took place. A one-world government took ownership of all the countries and implemented a digital currency. That was how they controlled people, initially, through a phone app. Then doctors implanted the brain chip in people's skulls under the pretense of managing the economy. Once the neural link was inside people's heads, they rolled out the mark of the beast. Hell followed. There was no other way to describe it; nightmarish years steeped in persecution, suffering, and torture.

It began with destroying Bibles. They wanted anything of a religious nature on the internet purged, like Christian blogs, devotionals, stories, and testimonials.

Then the burning of print books began. It was easier to burn all books than to sort through those that were Christian and those that weren't. Jace's wife had purchased many religious texts, and Jace, being a good citizen of the New World Order, purged every book from the house and took them to the tax collector's office. The collection center reimbursed his property taxes for the following year, which allowed him to keep his home a while longer. When he lost his job selling boats, he couldn't pay the mortgage or taxes.

He asked himself, "What would I give to have that Bible I gave to the tax collector?" Everything he once treasured, like his boat, was in a trash heap somewhere. The water was gone, so nobody needed a canoe or a dinghy. "Meaningless, meaningless," Jace muttered.

He remembered when pastors preached about survival. It was a different kind of survival called salvation. In this new world, the NWO forbade certain trigger words like "Jesus." 5G listening devices were everywhere, so if you uttered his name, drones would come after you. Jace had seen what the drones did to people. It was impossible to talk about God, listen to a sermon, or read Scripture. Even if you quoted a Bible passage in the privacy of your home, somehow, the globalists knew.

Jace couldn't remember when the worst part began, but when it did, everything changed. Without the mark, you couldn't function in society. It was worse than the infamous ESG scores in China. These new contrivances worked on steroids. The drones hunted down everyone who refused to receive the mark and killed them. And that's when Jace knew the truth. Emma was right. Aliens had not taken them; God raptured them, and he fled into the Ocala National Forest.

While Jace embraced some Biblical truths, he wasn't sure about others. He knew the mark of the beast was true. He had lived through that nightmare. Emma warned him, "If you get left behind, don't take the mark." But could everything else in the Bible regarding prophecy be true?

Jace sat beside the dried-up riverbed, feeling useless and unimportant. Who cared if he died? The survivalist set up his tiny one-person tent and crawled into his sleeping bag. What would he give for running water, a cup of coffee, and some decent food? Fortunately, in Florida, there were insects, dandelions, and succulents to eat when the hunger pangs became unbearable.

His mental funk was debilitating, so Jace crawled out of his sleeping bag and set up his small ham radio and antenna. He had charged the solar panels earlier. The radio was his only link to the outside world. He turned the dial to listen, but there was nothing except static.

Jace had not seen a human being or heard anyone's voice on the radio in months. It had been a shorter time since he heard someone sending Morse Code, but he didn't have his straight key to reply to the sender—it quit working a long time ago—and it probably would have been stupid to respond anyway. The government would have tracked down the signal, and since he didn't have the mark, a drone would have sought him out and killed him.

Still, hearing CW on the radio assured him that at least one other human being was alive. The CW operator sent CQ, CQ, CQ, followed by his call sign and the words, "I haven't seen anyone in over a year."

Jace thought about the fish he used to catch. Unlike their quick end, he felt himself bleeding out, painfully, a little bit at a time, aware that there was nothing he could do to stop it.

That night, he dreamed he was in a desert and desperately needed water. When all hope seemed lost, an oasis of percolating water shot up from the sands. "Oh, if I could only reach it," he whispered, but he was too weak. As he lay in the sand, breathing his last, water droplets edged closer. An unfamiliar sound startled him awake.

He got up on his haunches and looked out the tent. Was he dreaming? Next to the dried-up riverbed, a man was cooking fish over an open fire. Jace recognized the smell of crappie. Should he stay hidden in the tent or meet the visitor?

It didn't take him but a few seconds to decide. The smell of fresh fish on the open fire was a lure he couldn't resist, and to see another human being was surreal.

He stepped out of the tent, speaking as he approached the fisherman. "Hi, I'm Jace."

The man looked up and motioned, "Sit, and I will give you fish."

The visitor had deep-set brown eyes with a head covering framing his face, and he wore a white robe tied around the waist. His clothing was not American, although his Floridian accent was familiar. Right now, Jace didn't care about any of that. All he cared about was food.

The man handed Jace a large container of water, and Jace drank every last ounce of it. Then he felt guilty. He should have saved some for the man who offered it to him.

The stranger gave Jace all the fish, saving none for himself. When Jace was full, the foreigner said, "You've been in this wasteland for five years. If I include you, the remnant of believers in Florida might be several thousand."

He seemed to be hinting at Jace's indecisiveness. While he had not received the mark described in the Bible, he had not fully embraced Jesus as his Savior. Jace was a survivalist.

"The word of God is even rarer than the remnant," the visitor shared. "There might be a couple of thousand Bibles hidden in the United States—in strange places, but none near you."

"Who are you?" Jace asked.

The stranger didn't answer his question but asked Jace one. "Remember your dream?"

Jace nodded, perceiving the man must be an angel in disguise.

"I gave you spring water for your physical thirst, but what about your spiritual thirst?"

"What do you mean?" Jace asked, but he knew the answer before he even asked the question.

The angel replied, "I must go. Even though the days have been cut short, two years remain."

Jace threw his hands in the air. "Two years of this living hell?"

The supernatural creature nodded.

"This is how it all ends?" Jace asked again.

The angel shook his head. "No, Jace, this is not how it all ends. "The Lord wants to give you living water. The water I gave you is only temporary. It's passing away. You need the living water for salvation."

Jace knew the angel's purpose was singular, and God's patience must be running out. Jace admitted when he drank the spring water he saw the goodness of the Lord despite all the desolation.

"Will I survive two more years?" Jace asked. "Will I make it? Please tell me."

The angel seemed saddened that Jace asked the question. "Exercise your free will."

Could he survive two more years? Did he even want to?

Jace thought about his wife and daughter. He missed them so much. What would it be like to see them again? If God could find him in this uninhabited wasteland where he had avoided capture, God must be who he says he is in the Bible. Jace bowed and uttered the words that would change his future. "Forgive me, Jesus. I believe."[1]

6

WHAT IF

Ephesians 5:16 (NKJV)

...redeeming the time because the days are evil.

Adorned with gems like the heavenly Jerusalem, the Garden of Destiny glistened with intense, captivating charm. Mabel McNally waited in the garden as a spirit not yet born.

"I hope this baby becomes all God creates her to be," Gabriel said.

Castiel, the future guardian of Mabel, sighed. "God calls everyone to serve him, but few choose to do so."

The angels watched God wrap Mabel under the shadow of his wings. God's blessings and promises to all humankind were outward manifestations of his unconditional love for each one.

Castiel pondered all these things in his heart. "So many rewards for the earthlings, particularly this one. Her future will be difficult, starting with birth."

"We must pray," Gabriel said.

Castiel lamented. "I wish we knew the outcome for her and others because we love our assignments just as God loves us. We guide humans away from evil, fighting off demons and fallen angels, but our adversary is powerful. He taunts them in unimaginable ways."

Gabriel interrupted Castiel. "You must not think about the adversary. Instead, focus on the power God has given you to guide your assignment. Pray for her as Jesus prayed while he walked on the earth. Humans are weak at best."

Castiel nodded. "Yes, Gabriel. You, who spoke to Mary about the birth of the Messiah, you know so much more than me."

Gabriel reassured Mabel. "Remember your name, 'my cover is God,' and let God's Spirit guide you as the guardian of Mabel. She is a tough assignment, but God puts his strongest angels where they're most needed."

"Gabriel," Castiel said, "I've had the privilege of watching many earthlings who did not receive all the wonderful blessings God wanted to bestow upon them. Grief overwhelms me when I witness the mess humans make of their lives because of their fallen nature. If only they knew what wonderful gifts God has for them and what rewards he'll bless them with if they're faithful till the end. If only they knew."

Recognition of Castiel's sadness affected Gabriel deeply. "Castiel, if God had wanted to make humankind robots, he would have done so. God chose to give human beings free will. Jesus died for all humankind so they would not be robots. His gift on the cross allows for free will. He even died for those he knew would reject him. What kind of sacrificial love is that?"

Castiel shook his head. "I don't understand that kind of love, Gabriel. It's amazing, isn't it?"

"We must remember that," Gabriel said. "He died for all humans so they could choose whether to accept his love. Robots can't do that, and Jesus wanted a human family on earth, not robots."

Castiel added, "Jesus even separated himself from God on the cross and descended into hell."

"What is even more amazing," Gabriel said, "is he would have done it for only one human. That is how much he wanted a human family on earth."

"Gabriel," Castiel said, "it's beyond angelic understanding, and I feel powerless sometimes."

"Castiel," Gabriel affirmed, "God has given you all the power you need to influence your human for the kingdom of heaven. The choice ultimately belongs to Mabel."

Castiel sighed again. "Thank you, Gabriel, for reminding me of these eternal truths."

———

One Year Later

Mary McNally lay on the table at the abortionist's clinic to eliminate the "mass of cells" inside her body. She had just started college, and following a one-night fling with a freshman two months into her first semester, she found herself pregnant.

Having a baby was not part of her college plans. She had earned a full scholarship—hard to come by these days—and she wasn't about to lose it. She would be the first in her family to graduate from college. What would her parents say if they found out she was pregnant? The shame would be unbearable.

The nurse spoke to her. "Are you ready?"

Mary nodded. "I want to get this over with as quickly as possible. I have tests in a few days."

The anesthetist injected the medication into the IV to put her to sleep. Mary never woke up.

————

Castiel, Mabel's guardian angel, watched with heavenly joy as Mabel's new parents signed the adoption papers in the judge's chambers.

"Congratulations," Judge Hawkins said.

Eileen smiled as she held Mabel in her arms. After ten years of barrenness, she was a mother.

"Thank you, Jesus," she whispered in her heart. Castiel saw tears in the new mother's eyes. Mabel had survived a botched abortion even though her birthmother died. This little one had a fighting chance now when so many others didn't.

Castiel prayed, "Dear Jesus, please help this little one to increase in wisdom and stature and to find favor with both God and man."

Years passed, and Castiel watched over his human charge with every ounce of strength God gave him. After much prayer, Mabel accepted Jesus into her heart when she turned twelve.

As Castiel had prayed, Mabel grew in wisdom and stature. Her salvation was assured, but now it was up to the new convert to earn rewards for the kingdom. Accepting Jesus at such a young age meant she had a lifetime to follow the King and to find favor with God and man.

However, when Mabel turned sixteen, something happened that would change the course of her future—not only on earth but for eternity.

———

Sunlight pierced the windowpanes of Mabel's parents' bedroom, making the room exceptionally bright on a Sunday afternoon in May. Mabel's dad had asked her to bring all the passports to him as he was planning a summer vacation and wanted to make sure none needed renewal. "Look in the top drawer," he told her.

She shuffled through a large stack of papers, looking for the blue passports, when she came upon an envelope that read on the outside, "Adoption Papers."

"What is this?" Mabel muttered. She opened the envelope, and inside, she couldn't believe what the document said. She was adopted.

———

Mabel waved the adoption papers in front of her parents. "Why didn't you tell me?"

Shocked by her anger, the couple stared at their daughter. At last, her mother spoke. "What difference does it make, Mabel? We love you, and God gave you to us. It's not like you can search for your birth mother. She died at the hands of the abortionist."

"But you didn't tell me," Mabel said. "And I never knew I almost died in a botched abortion. Isn't that sort of important?" She threw the adoption papers at them and stormed out of the room.

———

Castiel shared the incident with Gabriel. "What can I do? The young girl is treading on bitter waters for not knowing her personal story and is angry that her parents withheld that information from her."

Gabriel listened attentively to Castiel.

"The evil one has found a foothold on the girl. Despite praying for the young maiden, I can't make a difference anymore. She no longer reads her Bible or attends the youth group at church. She is treading among snakes and vipers."

Sorrow filled Gabriel's heart as he pondered all these things. "We must pray, Castiel. Jesus bestows salvation on all who receive him, but rewards are earned. Her rewards are enormous."

"Indeed," Castiel said. "So much potential. Her testimony would bring many into the kingdom. I shall do everything I can to encourage her to do these things you mention—read her Bible, pray, go to church, and love the Lord with all her heart. The evil one knows her value for the kingdom of God and is doing everything he can to usurp God's calling on her life."

The two angels prayed for a long time. Following the conversation with Gabriel, Castiel pressed in hard as Mabel's guardian, but he also had to accept the young girl's free will, and the ultimate choice was hers. Castiel longed to see her enter the gates of heaven. He had taken a peek at her Book of Remembrance containing God's promises if she followed the straight and narrow path—but would she?

———

Sixty Years Later

Castiel often thought about the difference in time between earth and the third heaven. Season upon season passes until humans grow old and wonder where all the time went. In heaven, time has little significance. What seemed like decades to Mabel was only a fraction of that time to Castiel.

The day arrived when Mabel said goodbye to her friends and family. She closed her eyes and breathed her last, and Castiel, faithfully serving Jesus throughout Mabel's life, escorted her to the gates of heaven.

In her spiritual body, Mabel asked, by way of thought, "Where am I going?"

Castiel towered above Mabel, who was only 5'4". As Mabel locked onto Castiel's eyes, he anticipated heavenly knowledge filling her mind. He didn't need to answer. The Father would. Mabel's eyes bulged as God revealed uncomfortable truths.

———

Mabel peered longingly beyond the guarded entrance. She saw the splendor of the heavenly city, humans that shimmered in holy garments, and joy radiating from their faces. Then she saw her mother and father. Smiling, they waved and approached, but someone stepped in front of them. She looked into his eyes, magnificent eyes that emanated perfect love, a love so heavenly she couldn't describe it. Only her parents exhibited that kind of love when she was young, and sadness filled her heart because she had rejected it.

She remembered how everything changed when she turned 16. She thought about her soul's bitterness, the anger that burned within her, and how she clung to it. She chose not to forgive but to live in self-righteousness, pretending to be a victim. At that moment, Mabel realized the gift of salvation she received when she was twelve never blossomed into anything meaningful for God's kingdom.

The Savior loved her, an unconditional love that would linger in her mind for all eternity, but that unconditional love would not change her eternal future. Mabel sensed the Savior asking her, "What gifts do you have to give me?"

Mabel broke into tears. "This is all my fault," she moaned, and her physical strength left. She collapsed at the heavenly gates, knowing she would never enter them.

As she sat weeping, the Savior showed her all the magnificent rewards he had put away for her. She saw her promised place at the heavenly banquet and a shimmering, spotless gown reserved for her. Mabel witnessed the heavenly mansion Christ built for her and saw the millions of faithful followers she could have joined.

Mabel saw all of this in a fleeting moment. Then, Jesus turned his loving eyes away and moved on as redeemed earthlings followed him where she could not go.

Mabel turned to Castiel, "What's happening to me now?"

Castiel said, "Follow me."

"Where are you taking me?" Mabel asked. "Does this mean I go to hell?"

Castiel shook his head. "No, Mabel. You can't lose your salvation, only rewards."

Mabel breathed a sigh of relief. She wouldn't spend eternity in hell, but if she didn't go to heaven and she didn't go to hell, where would she go?

Once they were beyond the heavenly gates and the light of Jesus, Mabel could no longer see into the Kingdom of Light. Surrounded by thick darkness, she heard the voices of others but could not see them. Above the voices, she heard what sounded like weeping and gnashing of teeth.

Mabel's voice cracked. "Where are we?" As she spoke, her teeth chattered one against another. Recognizing the enormity of what she had lost, she had no one to blame but herself. She was a victim of her own poor choices.

"Is there anything in the kingdom for me?" Mabel asked. "Does Jesus have a gift for me?"

"Mabel," Castiel said, "you accepted Jesus as your Savior when you were twelve. That's his gift to you. Therefore, God's grace saved you from damnation. But you squandered your life for the kingdom. You have no rewards, no place in the heavenly city. You will live here, on the outskirts of the heavenly Jerusalem, mourning what you could have had, but you will never see hell. Here is the abode of those who have earned no rewards but who did accept Jesus as their Savior."

Mabel heard so much crying and teeth chattering it disturbed her. And then her teeth gnashed against each other as she wept for what she could have had. The worst part was that she saw the loving eyes of Jesus look away.

No amount of repentance would change her future. For the first time, she thanked her parents. At least here, there was thankfulness for salvation. If her parents had not been Christians, she probably would have gone to hell instead of the lowest place in heaven. Mabel acknowledged that darkness was a better place to live than in hellfire and torment.

"It is time for me to leave, Mabel," Castiel said. "I have been given a new assignment now that you have arrived at your place of eternal destiny."

Mabel wanted to cling to him, but she knew that was impossible. She watched as her guardian angel entered the bright light of the heavenly Jerusalem—a light she could not endure.

As Mabel's eyes adjusted to the darkness, she saw souls wandering in the eternal night, saved by the grace of God. She had sealed her fate and would spend eternity here left to ponder, what if?

1

7

LIFE IS NOT FAIR

Jeremiah 29:11 (NKJV)

For I know the thoughts that I think toward you, says
the Lord, thoughts of peace and not of evil, to give
you a future and a hope.

Life is not fair.

ope walked out of the courthouse, tired and hungry. After a three-hour deposition filled with too much banter between irate lawyers, she wanted to grab a bite to eat before heading home. While 24-hour rush jobs for court reporters paid well, when unexpected, they sucked. How many times had a rush job bashed her plans for the evening? But at least tonight, she had no plans.

The quickest dinner would be takeout Chinese food. Hope went to Kung Fu near her condo and bought some orange chicken and rice. Kung Fu always added a free fortune cookie. After eating most of her meal, she opened the fortune. On a small slip of paper inside the cookie were the words, "Life is not fair."

"What kind of fortune is that?" Hope muttered. "What does that mean?"

She thought about the clinic she drove by on the way home and the women waiting outside. Was it fair that the babies in those mothers' wombs would never see the light of day, feel a mother's breath on their face, or know what it was like to be loved? Hope lamented, "Those babies will die because their mothers don't want them."

She remembered the panhandlers who came up to her car begging for money as she sat at the red light. Had life been fair to them? Probably not. They would likely say life had not only been unfair but unkind. The idea that life wasn't fair had never struck Hope in such a profound way.

Over the next few days, the idea of life not being fair became an obsession. She saw how hard some people worked and earned only minimum wage. Was that fair? Perhaps the workers could make more if they went to school or received training in a skill. But maybe they didn't have the money, intelligence, or opportunity to do that.

When Hope drove by the hospital, she thought about all the patients undergoing treatment for various ailments, like cancer and heart disease, and names of diseases she couldn't even pronounce.

One day, after succumbing to depression over her inability to understand how anyone could be happy, she went to the beach. Stashed in her bag was bread to feed the seagulls. Hope noticed one seagull was lame, but he pushed his way through the crowd of anxiety-driven birds and snatched a couple of crumbs. His tenacity inspired Hope, and she tried harder to get the crumbs to him. When the bread was gone, the lame bird hobbled off with bread crumbs filling his happy belly.

"Maybe there is more to this 'it's not fair' thing than meets the eye," Hope said as she climbed into her car. Was it fair that the poor bird had an accident? Maybe he was in a fight. Perhaps he was born that way. Did it matter how he got hurt?

Hope noted the lame seagull wasn't sitting around feeling sorry for himself; he was surviving. He fought with every ounce of strength he possessed against all the odds stacked against him—because he lived in an unfair world.

Hope's thoughts returned to mothers who didn't want their babies. What chance did a helpless babe have at the scalpel of a skilled surgeon? She couldn't be sure, but she had heard that the doctors did their deed while the baby was still alive. Once a body dies, the organs die almost immediately. Now she was more depressed. Some circumstances provided no hope and no future. It wasn't fair. In fact, it was worse than unfair. It was inhumane.

Hope focused on the seagull again. Life had dealt the bird a devastating blow, but he chose to make the best of it. Was he just lucky that he had survived?

The luck of the draw, that's what it was. How depressing, though, to believe life was nothing more than karma. Some people receive good karma, and some people receive bad karma. Hope shook her head. "No, that can't be true. There must be something that controls the world besides karma and luck."

The idea of life being nothing more than a series of chances bothered Hope. "So, does that mean you cast your dreams upon the waters and hope one of them comes true?" Hope shook her head again. "If that were so, that would mean life was just a chasing after the wind."

Trying to make sense of it, Hope argued, "If everything that happens is just by chance, what difference does it make what kind of person you are? You can be a good person and have bad luck, or you can be a bad person and have good luck."

That thought alone made Hope angry. She wanted justice, but, as the fortune cookie said, "Life is not fair."

One day Hope decided to make a sandy butterfly way station for new monarch butterflies. She had seen the butterfly garden at Epcot and remembered how the butterflies would emerge sticky wet after undergoing a metamorphosis from the chrysalis. They would seek a place to dry off before heading into the sky on their magical journey across thousands of miles. She put sand in a dry birdbath with several small rocks. Then she put the birdbath next to where she had planted milkweed for the butterflies.

But Hope forgot about her butterfly way station in the birdbath. A few weeks later, the forgotten birdbath caught her attention. She noticed the summer rains had filled it, and no butterflies could use it because rainwater covered the rocks.

However, as she peered into the water, she saw hundreds of things moving around. What were those wiggly bugs? When she examined the tiny creatures more closely, she realized they were tadpoles. A mother frog must have found the birdbath and decided to lay her eggs there; hundreds had hatched.

What was Hope going to do with all those tadpoles? Life would be unfair to them if she dumped them on the deck. That would be unkind, even cruel.

Perhaps life wasn't just about being fair or unfair. A friend had recently died, so in honor of her friend, she wanted to release the tadpoles into a nearby lake, much like people release balloons into the sky. That would bring redemption out of sadness, save the tadpoles, and make her feel good that she did something for some tiny critters who could do nothing for themselves.

A week later, Hope took the tadpoles to the lake, said a few kind words about her friend who had passed away, and released them. A feeling of satisfaction swept over her. The tadpoles would grow into frogs—those that didn't get eaten—and someday have baby tadpoles themselves.

And the circle of life would continue—at least for them.

Then Hope had a new revelation. The fortune cookie said life wasn't fair, but that didn't mean she couldn't make a difference. Hope had free will. She could accept the fortune cookie's proclamation that life wasn't fair and live her life in that vein, or she could choose to make the world a better place. And while that seemed like a lofty goal, was it enough? Or was there more to contentment than simply doing good things? She longed for something bigger than her dreams, abilities, and expectations.

One day she was at a basketball game, and one of the players committed a foul. He argued the call with the referee, and the referee tossed the player from the competition. Then the player's coach came out and contested the same call, and the referee threw the coach out of the game.

"So, who referees our lives?" Hope asked. Someone or something had to be in charge. If there were referees to manage basketball games, there had to be a referee or referees to control the world or the entire universe.

Even in a basketball game, somebody kept a record of how many shots a player made, how many fouls he committed, and how many assists he had. If officials did that in a meaningless ballgame, somebody must keep score in the bigger game of life.

Hope accepted that life wasn't fair, but sooner or later, things that weren't fair had to be reconciled, just like her checkbook had to be balanced. She had recently learned about the importance of that when she overdrew her account because of a silly mistake. However, the bank didn't see it that way—they charged her over a hundred dollars for three overdrafts.

There had to be a reckoning in this unfair world. Maybe that's what Hope longed for, judgment. Then she asked, "Who determines what is fair or unfair?" Hope recalled the basketball game and the ref who threw out the player and the coach. Only an impartial referee could do that.

Could there be a divine being who called the shots, ensured justice was carried out, and fixed those things that weren't fair? What about all the wicked people who did evil things? There had to be a God who weighed the good and the bad, who someday would assess everything that everybody had ever done.

One day Hope was working as a court reporter in a trial that lasted for several days. The judge called a lunch break, and she went to a nearby restaurant to enjoy the much-needed time off. Following lunch, when she returned, she knew her job would be taxing. The defense had brought in an expert witness from out of state, which meant it would be tedious with multiple direct and cross-examinations. She thought about the jury and their task—to decide if the plaintiffs had proven their case. Sometimes it was hard to know where the truth was, and she didn't envy their job. All she did as a court reporter was write down what was said and certify that it was accurate.

Soon she returned to the courthouse and took her seat in front of the judge. The defense began their direct examination, which went on for a while. As she sat close to the witness to write his testimony, she noticed that he started having a medical issue, perhaps a seizure, but nobody else initially noticed.

It became apparent to everyone in the courtroom when he passed out on the witness stand. At first, nobody did anything. How often did witnesses die in the middle of an examination?

Someone called an ambulance, the bailiff escorted the jury out, and the judge called a recess.

———

The legal system is supposed to be about fairness. You get into trouble, and somebody sues you. You've been a victim and want compensation. You hope the system treats you fairly.

Death has a way of stopping everything. That day everything seemed meaningless. Was it fair that the expert witness had diabetes and died on the witness stand? Of course, the judge was powerless to save the man. He was just the judge of the trial and not of the man's life.

The question continued to linger in Hope's heart. Was there a judge over life and death? Or did everything happen by chance? She reasoned that there must be a supreme being somewhere. Otherwise, people would be mere puppets on a string and only able to respond when someone pulled their string.

Hope shook her head. "No, I don't believe that," she said. "I'm not a puppet. I have free will to decide how I will react to the unfairness of life. That's a good thing." She thought about that fortune cookie she had opened several months earlier that said, "Life is not fair." Because she had free will, she had chosen a higher moral path to do good things because she wanted to.

One day Hope was shopping, and nature called. She needed to make an unexpected visit to the ladies' room. As she squatted over the toilet, she saw a pamphlet on the door with a beautiful monarch butterfly. Underneath the photo was the question, "Are you born again?"

Was it a coincidence? She remembered her monarch butterfly garden full of milkweed and her failed attempt to provide a sandy way station for them when they emerged from the chrysalis. Tadpoles were born instead, and she took them to the lake so they could grow into frogs.

She pulled the pamphlet off the door to read all of it. Suddenly, she understood. Just as caterpillars and tadpoles had to be "born again" to become butterflies and frogs, people must be born spiritually to become the man or woman God called them to be.

Why had nobody explained this to her? Or perhaps she had

closed her eyes, ears, and heart to this simple truth. Now that God had given her a divine revelation, she wanted to find a Bible. She wanted to learn more about the Creator, the referee of the universe, the one who gave her free will.

In the bathroom stall, after poring over the words in the pamphlet, Hope committed her life to Jesus Christ. How would anyone believe she locked herself in a public, smelly bathroom to pee and then emerge cleansed from all unrighteousness? Probably no one except another born-again Christian—and monarch butterflies and frogs.

Hope reflected. If she could be born again, aborted babies would be born again too—somehow, some way. She hoped that was the case, but for today, God had healed her heart. The fortune cookie had only conveyed a half-truth. Even if life isn't fair, as a born-again Christian, she could choose a higher calling than just being a good person. She could live for the glory of God even in an unfair world.[1]

8

RANSOM SMITH

Proverbs 9:14-17 (NKJV)

For she sits at the door of her house, on a seat by the highest places of the city, to call to those who pass by, who go straight on their way: "Whoever is simple, let him turn in here"; and as for him who lacks understanding, she says to him, "Stolen water is sweet..."

The successful businessman reveled in the applause. He had worked hard for this prestigious award. Everyone admired his strong work ethic, determination, and that he had saved the failing tech giant from a humiliating fall. The major news outlets featured his accomplishments, and *Time* magazine named him a finalist in the "Businessman of the Year" award. That was the award that had eluded him for too long.

A pang of jealousy ripped through his heart. Mr. Ransom Smith personally knew the last two winners, and he was much more of a business genius than they were. He spit on the busy New York City street sidewalk as he pushed through the crowds. Remembering the night before, he repeatedly played the applause and accolades in his head.

Why couldn't his wife appreciate how wonderful he was? When he arrived home after a ten-hour day, the tired, haggard woman wasn't interested in his exploits. Even the cat ignored him. Only the dog appreciated the sacrifices he had made, wagging his tail and extending affectionate licks and kisses.

Mr. Smith approached a busy intersection he frequented several times during the week. One business establishment always caught his attention—The Utopia Connection. Business people frequented this hole in the wall, and today wasn't any different.

Two men entered as a stunning young woman greeted them with blonde hair draped over her shoulders in ringlets. Mr. Smith glanced at his iPhone. He had a few minutes to linger. Unexpectedly, as the blonde bombshell shut the door behind her customers, her eyes caught his. Ransom, surprised by the chance encounter, fixated on her face.

The young woman smiled. Her enticing eyes called to him, speaking to his soul, "Ransom, stolen water is sweet, and bread eaten in secret is pleasant...come and celebrate with me...."

The woman disappeared inside, and Mr. Smith shook his head, mumbling under his breath, "That was odd. It was as if she knew me. Maybe the young lady did know me. Maybe she had seen the news coverage. Maybe I should introduce myself."

The man stood and watched a couple more business people enter. He imagined it must be a restaurant and edged closer out of curiosity. How had he not noticed the grand entrance before—the mosaic-lined floor and the golden flower pots? Still, the strange photographs caught Ransom's attention the most.

Snapshots lined the walls with an assortment of captions, "Bill was here," "John's favorite hangout," "Sam's place," and dozens more. Ransom did not know any of the men. Strangely, Ransom noted that all the visitors were dead. Beneath their photographs were the dates of their untimely demises.

The scent of burning candles and air misters permeated the softly lit marquee. Etched glass lined the other wall. Mr. Smith tried to see through the exquisite façade but to no avail. He waited for someone to exit, to ask what was inside this beautiful, captivating establishment. After all, Ransom didn't want anyone to identify him entering a place that might be unseemly. He was too prideful to fall for that temptation. But despite his waiting longer than he wanted, no one exited.

It must be an extraordinary place, Mr. Smith reasoned, because so many enter and no one leaves. A few more minutes passed as Mr. Smith's curiosity clashed with his better judgment. He glanced at his watch. If he didn't go now, he would be late for his next meeting. But he longed to admire that beautiful face once more. He wanted to see those eyes, those eyes that latched onto his.

She no doubt knew him from the news reports, and if by some unlikely chance she didn't, he could impress her with his accomplishments. Surely, she would be impressed. *I wonder if she is married....*

Abruptly the door opened, and Mr. Smith was surprised to see only the beautiful young woman reappear. Where were the men? But he quickly dismissed the question as he peered into those eyes—deep and mysterious.

She held her hand to him, and once more, Ransom heard the exact words in his mind earlier: "Stolen water is sweet, and bread eaten in secret is pleasant."

"Yes," the man replied, "I'd love to share your stolen water and secret bread. And I'll pay."

He followed the young woman through the door and disappeared inside. The door shut behind him.

Mr. Ransom did not know the dead were there and her former guests were in hell.

9

OUT WITH THE OLD, IN WITH THE NEW

Galatians 5:4 (NKJV)

You have become estranged from Christ, you who
attempt to be justified by law; you have fallen
from grace.

"You win," Pastor Josh Johnson said as the tennis ball bounced into the corner.

"Ah," Rabbi Amos Aaronson exclaimed. "One more game?"

Josh shook his head as he felt sweat dripping down his face. "If we play another game, we'll be late for dinner." He imagined his fiancée Jill's disapproval if he presented for dinner without a shower. "Maybe someday I'll be good enough to beat you."

Josh walked over to retrieve the ball, and his hand froze. Flames engulfed the ball—at least on one side—and water encircled the other side. His heart skipped as he clenched his eyes, imagining he had cancer or some horrible disease. When he opened them, the ball looked normal.

He shook his head as if he could shake off the memory. Suddenly the game seemed meaningless. He picked up the ball and flitted his eyes about the court. Everything appeared normal. Maybe it was his imagination. After all, it had only lasted a few seconds. He convinced himself that's all it was.

He heard Amos laughing. "I had some lucky shots today."

Josh thought about Amos' words. Life was like that. Sometimes you were lucky or in the right place at the right time. Other times, you felt the hand of God with such assurance that you couldn't deny it was God. During those times, you knew it wasn't chance or luck. And then, sometimes, God gave people a word of knowledge—or even visions, right? Maybe he'd had one of those.

Josh reflected. Without Amos' friendship, he might not have become a Christian. As a teen, he was drawn to Amos because he was intrigued by his Jewish God. Of course, Jews didn't proselytize, but he and Amos had shared many adventures together in Boy Scouts. God must have kept them close friends all these years for a reason, but his witness for the Kingdom had been almost nonexistent. Josh felt badly about it, but sometimes the most important subjects were difficult to discuss with those whose friendships went deep.

Despite their religious differences, the men, in many ways, were alike. They were the same age, became engaged at the same time, and would marry within a week of each other in the not-too-distant future. The men looked like brothers with dark hair, brown eyes, and movie star looks.

Amos clasped Josh on the shoulder as the two tennis buddies headed to the showers. "Good game. What time are those dinner reservations?"

"Six. The girls will meet us there—with tables reserved." Josh chuckled. "They know we're always late after tennis."

———

After showering, the two men rode the gym elevator down to the lobby. When the door didn't open, Amos pushed the button. The elevator door seemed stuck. Josh looked at Amos, but neither said anything. Josh mused the gym needed to service it.

Impatient, Amos pushed the button a couple more times. When it finally opened, a bright light pierced the elevator darkness.

Josh whispered. "What's that?"

Amos' eyes met Josh's. "This isn't the lobby."

Josh stuck out his head. "This is insane."

The two men stepped out of the elevator into a vast heavenly-like garden. Josh recognized some of the flowers because his fiancée was a florist. Flowering trees and bushes filled the countryside as far as the horizon. Josh stooped down and picked up a prayer flower lying on the ground.

"This is Jill's favorite flower," he said and stuck it in his pocket. They weren't in season now, so she would wonder where he found it.

Amos, timider than Josh, followed behind his friend. As they walked, Josh heard a swish and glanced behind them. The men exchanged looks. The elevator was gone. Without that, they couldn't get back.

Before either of them could say anything, a towering figure, clothed in bright light, materialized.

The two men scampered back.

"Fear not," the figure said, "And welcome to the King's garden."

"The King's garden?" Josh repeated.

"Who are you?" Amos asked.

"I'm a heavenly messenger, and the King has sent me to deliver three important messages to Rabbi Amos Aaronson."

Josh and Amos exchanged glances. "An angel," Josh whispered.

The supernatural being handed Amos three sealed scrolls. Josh leaned into Amos to get a better look.

Glancing at his Jewish friend, Josh asked the messenger, "Can he open them now?"

"Soon," the messenger said. "You will notice each scroll has a number on the seal. You can open the first scroll at the appointed time. After the first encounter, you can break the second seal, and after the second encounter, you can break the third seal."

Josh had no idea what the angel meant. "What's an encounter? An encounter with what?"

"And how will we know?" Amos asked.

Josh sensed fear wrapping its tentacles around his buddy.

"Fear not," the messenger said. "Make sure you follow the path. Do not deviate to the right or the left, lest you're tempted to go astray and become lost."

As quickly as the messenger appeared, he disappeared. Josh and Amos stared at each other. Neither said anything until Josh broke the silence, "We should have asked if we're supposed to break the seal before we follow the path."

"Let's break the first one," Amos said. He handed the scroll to Josh. "Here, you do it."

"On second thought, I think we should wait."

Amos chuckled. "When is the appointed time? A good rabbi always follows the law."

Josh nodded. "We'll take the path to the destination and break the seal."

"Okay. Perhaps that's the best thing."

Josh returned the scroll to his friend, and Amos stuck it in his pocket.

"Besides," Josh said, "the angel handed you the scrolls, not me. I think you should open them."

Amos shrugged. "Well, there is only one path, so I don't think we'll get lost."

The two men started along the trail through the garden, and Josh took note of the sun shining above them in the cloudless sky. How reassuring that seemed now. The familiarity eased his fear, and he remembered the vision earlier of the fiery tennis ball on the court. Did that have anything to do with this?

As the two men walked, a breeze caressed their faces. Butterflies danced around the flowers, and Josh imagined the elegant insects whispering praises in the wind. Joyful songs filled his ears as colorful birds darted overhead. Sweet aromas drifted by. His fiancée would love this place, Josh mused.

The path meandered over small hills and valleys, a good walk, though not tiring. Josh almost hated for it to end, but as they approached what might have been a final hill, laughter piqued his interest.

"That sounds like the girls," Amos said.

Josh pointed. "It's coming from over there, I think."

"No, I think it's that way," Amos said.

The two men listened again.

The girls' laughter ebbed and flowed. "I know that's Ann and Jill," Amos said. "Look, there's a path we can take. Let's go find them."

Josh hesitated. "The messenger told us not to leave the trail, that we might get lost."

"Well," Amos said, "there is only this trail we're walking on and that one. I don't think we're going to get lost." He chuckled. "Come on, let's go find them."

Josh liked Amos' enthusiasm. Besides, what a fantastic place to share with the one you will soon marry. "Okay. We'll bring them along on this amazing adventure."

The two men took off on the side trail listening for the girls' voices, which seemed fainter now, but still audible. So as not to lose them, they hurried faster until the path ended.

"I don't hear them now," Amos said.

Josh noticed something odd. "The trail we took to get here has disappeared."

The rabbi threw up his hands. "That can't be."

But sure enough, the trail they had walked along with such enthusiasm was overgrown with flowers.

Amos shook his head. "I think we're in trouble."

"We shouldn't have left the path the messenger told us to take," Josh said. As a pastor, though, he had to take some responsibility. He couldn't blame it all on Amos.

Amos surveyed the rolling hills captivated with flowers. "Well, there are worse places to get lost."

Josh felt convicted. "Amos, there is something supernatural going on." Josh closed his eyes and prayed. When they finished, the messenger stood before the two men.

"Why did you leave the trail?" he asked.

"We heard the voices of Anne and Jill," Amos said.

The messenger admonished them. "How quickly the evil one led you astray. If you are so easily deceived, what about the flock you lead? How can you guide them on the straight and narrow path?"

Josh knew the messenger was right. He knew from the beginning they should've stayed on the trail. "Can you help us get back?"

The messenger turned his focus to Amos. "According to the Torah, do you get a second chance when you sin?"

Amos squirmed. "The law reveals our sin."

"And our inability to follow it," Josh added.

The messenger admonished both men again. "The evil one means this for evil, but God means it for good."

"I'm sorry," Josh said as he looked up into the heavens.

At once, the hidden trail reappeared, and the messenger was gone.

"How does he do that?" Amos asked

Josh gazed at where the messenger had stood only seconds before. "I don't know."

———

The men took the side trail back and continued on the one they shouldn't have left. Soon Josh's gloominess lifted as the words of the messenger comforted him. It was time he heeded the advice he gave to others; focus on the process and not the outcome.

A half-hour passed when a booming voice commanded, "Remove your shoes. You're standing on holy ground."

With fear and trepidation, Josh removed his tennis shoes, and

Amos removed his sandals. Josh remembered the story of Moses and the burning bush.

"Let's keep going," Josh said, leading the way. "God has something to show us."

Soon they came to a large door on the path. Nothing held it in place, but it appeared to be secure.

"Why is there a door here?" Amos asked.

The door appeared to be open and closed at the same time. Josh could not understand how both could be true, but he could partially see through the door. Despite that, something prevented them from entering. Josh touched the doorframe, rubbing his fingertips across it. It wasn't an illusion, but there was no way to open the door.

Amos glanced at his feet, remembering his Jewish history. "Josh, perhaps this is an invitation—the only reference in the Torah to a door is the door to the Holy Place.

"The voice said we were standing on holy ground...." Josh's voice trailed off. The door in the New Testament was a reference to Jesus. Maybe this was an invitation for Amos to witness to Josh, but as a Jew, Amos would never make the association of Jesus to the door. Josh had already shared Yeshua with Amos, and it seemed pointless to bring it up again.

"Let's see if we can find any clues," Josh said. "We must be missing something." He hoped the voice would speak again and give them direction, but only chirping birds filled his ears. After an exhaustive search—neither dared to step off the trail—they returned to where they started.

They tried to skirt around it once more, but something prevented them. Josh examined the door and noticed white cherubim covering the panels with shades of blue, purple, and scarlet threads. Despite that, he could still see through it—partially.

Josh debated whether to share that Jesus was the door. No matter how much he wanted to, he couldn't bring himself to do it. Not under these circumstances. Amos was already stressed—why stress him more with religious arguments he had long rejected?

Not knowing what to do, the two men sat in deep thought. Why were they here? Then Josh remembered the scrolls. How could they forget them so quickly? "Amos, we can break the first seal now."

Before proceeding, Amos checked the scroll number to make sure it was labeled one. When he opened it, he read the words out loud, "Expect a visitor."

"Expect a visitor," Josh repeated. He looked around. They were sitting in the middle of a vast garden next to a door. Was the message referring to the messenger who had rescued them? Or were they to look for another?

As these thoughts filled Josh's mind, he noted how tired he felt. He closed his eyes and prayed. "Dear Jesus, whoever the visitor is, make his identity clear." Josh had seen many Christians deceived by impostors, and the evil one had already led them down the wrong path. He didn't want to be fooled again.

As he prayed, Amos nudged him. "Look."

Josh opened his eyes. "A lamb?"

The unblemished white lamb meandered along the path, and Josh noticed the animal was carrying something. "What's on his back?"

"It's the Torah," Amos said.

As he removed it from the lamb's back, the volume and size of the Torah increased so dramatically that he couldn't hold it. Putting it on the ground would have been a transgression. So he took the massive book and propped it against the door. When he stepped back, the Torah increased in size until it covered the entrance. Amos bowed in the Jewish tradition, and Josh closed his eyes and prayed with him.

When they finished praying, the lamb was gone.

———

The Torah barred them from going through the door. Amos turned to Josh. "As a Christian, what do you think this means?"

"I think we should break the second seal," Josh said.

"Good idea." After doing so, Amos read the message to Josh. "Expect a visitor. Wait for him."

"The same message as before, it sounds like."

Amos retrieved the first scroll and held them up beside each other. "The message is the same." He handed them to Josh.

————

The sound of wood splintering filled the garden, and the Torah began to crack. The door looked like a jigsaw puzzle as pieces peeled away. A mighty wind blew, and more pieces fell on the ground.

Amos and Josh kept their distance as the wind swirled, and large gaping holes emerged in the door. Then the door completely faded away, and Yeshua stood clothed in a raiment of dazzling light. His appearance lasted for only a few seconds, and then he disappeared.

Josh didn't see his friend. "Amos?"

"I'm behind the rock."

Josh scrambled over to him. "Did you see Yeshua?"

Amos couldn't answer.

Josh touched his friend on the shoulder. "Remember what the messenger said?"

"Fear not—impossible."

"Amos, that was the Messiah. You don't need to hide from him. He is your hiding place."

Tears filled Amos's eyes. "Josh, I don't know what to think."

"We have one more scroll to unseal."

Amos lifted his eyes but remained silent.

"The scroll, Amos. Let's unseal the third scroll."

Amos pulled it out of his pocket and read it. "Enter the open door." He looked at Josh blankly.

"The door is Yeshua, Amos. As the Temple priests sacrificed the lambs on the altar, Jesus offered himself as the perfect lamb."

Amos shook his head. "Josh, I wish it were true. I mean, some of it makes sense, but—"

"But what?"

"—Jesus wasn't a Jew, and the Messiah must be Jewish."

"He was Jewish," Josh said. They had had this conversation before, but Amos interrupted his thoughts.

"What about all the Jews killed by Christians, like the Crusades, the Spanish Inquisition, and the Nazis? And what about Martin Luther and St. Augustine? Martin Luther was as anti-Semitic as they came. Hitler weaponized Martin Luther's writings to kill the Jews, leading to the Holocaust."

Amos glared at Josh. "St. Augustine might have been worse. He said God was finished with the Jews. Allegorizing the Bible, he said those promises were now for the Christians. Some Christians won't even mention the name Israel, calling the land Palestine," emphasizing the word "Palestine" as he spoke.

When Josh hesitated, Amos' tirade got worse. "You expect me to believe in Jesus after all of that? And in case you weren't aware, Christians accuse us of killing their Savior."

Amos appeared visibly shaken, and Josh feared his best friend might crack. No doubt, these feelings arose from deep within the rabbi, the result of others reminding him of these atrocities.

Josh pleaded with God, "I've yearned for this conversation for so long. Let not this moment pass without seeing my friend believe in Yeshua."

A breeze stirred, and Josh remembered the sordid history of the Christian church. Josh couldn't deny it nor refute it. Satan wanted to annihilate God's chosen people, and history proved that Christians did little to prevent their slaughter. If anything, they magnified it.

Josh knew God had not abandoned the Jews, and he never would. He prayed, "Jesus, help me."

Amos began to weep. "Josh, help me with my unbelief. I can't go through that door unless I believe Yeshua is who he said he was."

Josh placed his hand on Amos' shoulder. "Amos, Yeshua was Jewish."

"How do we know that?" Amos asked.

"Because we know Yeshua's genealogy. If you read Matthew and Luke in the New Testament, the writer recorded Jesus' genealogy through Mary and Joseph's lineage. Yeshua's ancestors came from the Tribe of Judah, so his heritage goes through King David back to Abraham."

"Really?" Amos asked, amazed that Josh knew that much about Judaism.

Josh nodded. "Yes. And think about this. The Romans destroyed all the historical records when they burned the Temple in 70 A.D. That means to have proof that the Messiah was Jewish, he needed to have been born before the destruction of the Temple. Otherwise, no proof of ancestry exists, and the Bible is clear the Messiah will come out of Judah."

Josh saw Amos' eyes light up at this revelation. "Amos, I can make no excuse for the actions of those who called themselves Christians and committed the most heinous crimes in history. Someday they'll have to account for their actions, but in no way is that a reflection on God."

Amos listened intently.

"Throughout history, Satan has tried to annihilate the Jews. That's because he knew salvation to the world would come through the Jews, so he did everything he could to thwart God's plan."

Josh changed tacks to keep his friend listening. "Think about it this way. In some ways, the first Holocaust was the crucifixion of Jesus."

"Christians blame the Jews for his death," Amos countered.

Josh shook his head. "No, Amos. The Jews didn't kill Jesus; the Romans didn't crucify him, either. The Bible says Yeshua died willingly, and legions of angels would have come to his rescue if he had asked."

"So why did Jesus allow wicked men to do what they did? Why didn't he save himself?"

Josh had hoped Amos would ask that question. "Because Yeshua needed to fulfill the Torah perfectly. He had to be sacrificed as the perfect lamb. He became sin so we could enter into his holy presence. Sin separates us from God. Yeshua laid down his life willingly because of love. God wanted a family on earth like he had a heavenly family. God needed a perfect sacrifice to atone for sin, and the only one who is perfect is Jesus."

"So you don't believe God has turned his back on the Jews?"

Josh shook his head. "If that were true, what assurance do I have that God won't renege on any of his promises? God is perfect. He keeps his promises."

"I don't think many Christians believe what you're saying, Josh. I've never heard this before."

"That may be true," Josh said sadly, "But the Scriptures are true. The Torah says God's promises to the Jews are eternal. The land of Israel belongs to the Jews, and the day is approaching when Yeshua will return and set up his throne in Jerusalem and reign for a thousand years."

"Seriously?" Amos asked.

"Seriously."

Amos looked at the open door.

Josh imagined what thoughts might be going through his friend's head. "Amos, that third scroll, why don't you reread it."

"Enter the open door." Without hesitating, Amos stood. "I'm ready."

As Josh and Amos passed through the door, praises filled the third heaven. The lion of the tribe of Judah sat on the throne, and millions praised and worshipped the King of Kings. As they gazed at the heavenly scene, Josh touched the prayer flower in his pocket. He couldn't wait to share the conversion of Amos with his fiancée when they returned.

10

COUNTERFEIT

2 Thessalonians 2:9 (NKJV)

The coming of the lawless one is according to the
working of Satan, with all power, signs, and lying
wonders...

The leaders of the New World Order sat eating lunch in the new Hanging Gardens of Babylon designed by Kai, a renowned horticulturist. Surrounded by tropical ferns, prickly succulents, meandering vines, and exotic flowers, they chatted about secret matters of which the commoners had no knowledge. Kai knew their secrets because the garden he created was their favorite hangout. He noted that while the rest of the world ate green —they ate meat and other delicacies he couldn't even identify.

The globalists valued Kai's knowledge only to satisfy their selfish ambitions. Kai was not significant except for his horticultural expertise, and he was ordered to keep what he knew a secret. That wasn't hard to do in the largely deserted city.

The plebeians, like Kai, had once been middle-class citizens. "Own nothing, and you'll be happy," the World Economic Forum touted. The globalists convinced the masses that a virtual world would be far more pleasant than the future world, which would not include animal meat, living in big houses, or driving gasoline-powered cars.

"We must ensure depopulation to meet sustainability. The future of humankind depends on our sacrifice," the elite claimed.

As Kai thought about their lies, he suppressed his anger only to perform his job. Then he would go home, turn on the computer, and escape. His virtual reality consisted of dozens of gardens worldwide. He had the benefit of both worlds—but was it a blessing or a curse?

Kai lamented. The masses probably couldn't even remember the fragrance of a rose. Living in ghost towns because of population depletion, they would return home each day from monotonous factory jobs, plug themselves into the computer, and escape into a virtual existence.

One of the guests waved his hand to get Kai's attention.

Kai walked over. "Can I help you?"

The man nodded. "Yes, I would like more wine."

Kai went to the bar. As he poured the drink, he saw his daily visitor, a white dog, eating some elderberries nearby. He had recently noticed the white dog limping, but today the animal seemed better. Kai knew the berries were good for inflammation, but how did the animal know that? The world-renowned horticulturist knew almost everything about every plant species and had planted medicinal specimens in the garden. Therapeutic drugs were only for the elite, but Kai knew of the healing powers in the leaves of plants.

After serving the wine, Kai returned to tending the garden. His mind wandered as he imagined some divine being speaking everything into existence. Now that God had given him this unique position, he made it his goal to protect every green thing he had painstakingly planted.

But there was a cost. Kai lived a lonely life. He knew too many "secrets." They would liquefy him if he shared that secret knowledge. The uncomfortable truth was that isolation caused by multiple pandemics created a lifestyle where commoners lived alone. Things didn't go well for those who complained. Liquefaction was how they eliminated humans who were troublemakers.

The white dog came over to Kai, and Kai leaned down to pat him on the head. "I should give you a name," Kai said, "but if I do, I will love you too much." He feared the elite would discover the animal and remove him from the garden. So Kai maintained his distance emotionally but longed to embrace the dog's love.

It was almost time for the rich rulers to depart, and Kai would close the garden and head home, eat his veggie meal, enjoy his allotted wine, and hook himself up to his computer. Before going to bed, he would enjoy a few hours in the gardens he had virtually designed.

Seeing that the dog no longer limped lifted Kai's spirits. He ran his hand along the dog's back. "I'm glad you're feeling better." Kai glanced in the direction of the restaurant guests. "Now go hide. They'll leave soon, and I don't want them to see you."

The dog brushed up against his legs and ran off. Kai smiled. The garden was not only a getaway for the globalists, but there were a few animals that had survived the war, and they made their homes here, too.

———

Later that evening, Kai parked before his computer, and his 3-D virtual reality sprung to life. Kai enjoyed traversing the gardens worldwide—gardens that no longer existed. Pollution, war, and plagues had decimated the grasslands and forests. His virtual world was the blueprint for recreating those gardens.

Tonight, though, his interest was superficial. Kai thought about the white dog who lived in the natural garden. The botanist yanked off the headphones and removed the 3-D glasses. Was this how he would live the rest of his life? If given a choice, which world would be better? No beauty existed now, no gardens—except the one he designed.

Virtual reality wasn't freedom; it was bondage. Despite Kai's preeminent position, he knew he would always be inferior to the globalists. They only wanted his knowledge.

What would he give to have the old world back? With its realness came love, joy, and the travails of experiential living, even if it was messy and unpredictable, at times, even painful. But sameness was dull. A virtual reality contained nothing but figments of one's imagination. Without realism, nothing was real—especially a virtual world that didn't exist.

———

The next day Kai went to the garden, and the white dog greeted him as usual. His appearance was reassuring, and Kai rewarded him with a treat. Afterward, the dog disappeared into the woods. Kai figured he wouldn't see him as much with his leg healed. That made him sad, but it also kept his best friend safe.

That afternoon, a truck pulled up to the garden gate. Kai saw an unusual tree in the cargo bed—a tree he could not identify. "I didn't order this tree," Kai said.

The delivery man handed him the purchase order.

Kai glanced at the paperwork. "I don't know this person." He watched as the delivery man set the tree on the curb, and then he left. Kai examined the tree's leaves. He knew every tree on the planet, or almost, and he did not recognize the species.

Later in the afternoon, Kai's boss arrived. "I bet you are wondering about the tree?"

Kai nodded, "Yes. I don't recognize the species."

"It's a brand-new creation, developed in the laboratory by our top scientists. The tree has a triple helix."

Kai blinked. "What?"

His boss laughed. "You heard me. Scientists have improved the double helix design and can't wait to propagate the tree. They selected this garden as the trial site because of your expertise. As you know, there are only a few gardens left. You must be thrilled."

Kai was speechless. Finally, he muttered, "I will keep you apprised."

His boss seemed pleased. "Good. You're an excellent record keeper, which is another reason why the elitists chose you. If this tree thrives, the geneticists plan to create hundreds of new species with the triple helix design. Perhaps it will replace all double helix life forms."

After a few more disturbing comments, Kai's boss left. Kai walked over to the triple helix. Sadness filled the gardener's heart. He had poured his life into what he hoped would regenerate the wastelands of the world, and his garden was about to be destroyed by an invasive, artificial species.

As he moved the tree to a more permanent location, his boss returned. "I forgot to mention, scientists created the tree in the lab under low light conditions, so be gentle with the sunlight."

"Okay," Kai said.

As his boss requested, he moved the tree away from the others into the shadows. He also didn't want to contaminate the habitat if it had any parasites or diseases. He set up a file for the tree, meticulously entering the data into the computer.

Three days passed. Kai checked the tree each day. But he noticed when he was near it that it felt like the tree was watching him, or was it just his imagination?

He also noted that the white dog would not go near the triple helix tree. He went out of his way to give a wide berth to it. And the trees next to the triple helix were no longer thriving. Fallen leaves littered the ground leaving some of the branches bare. Concerned, Kai moved the triple helix farther away to protect the precious trees he had raised from saplings.

Nighttime approached, and Kai was running late. As he made his final round in the darkening garden, the dog was reluctant to accompany him. Usually, the white dog followed Kai, wagging his tail, as Kai checked on plantings and secured the building. Kai shrugged. Maybe his leg was bothering him again.

When he checked the triple helix, he noticed something odd. What was that dark strand on the trunk of the tree? He approached it to get a better look, and something lunged out at him and bit him on the cheek."

Kai writhed in pain. Petrified, he watched as a snake slithered up the trunk. The third strand of the tree's DNA was a snake!

Horror filled him as the pain increased. He ran his finger over the injury, and blood covered his fingertips. He hurried inside the building to examine the puncture wound. When he looked in the mirror, relief filled his mind. The fang mark was small and shouldn't be noticeable in a couple of days. But how much poison had entered his body? He knew the snake was venomous because whatever the globalists did was toxic. Did the dog know something he didn't know?

He walked outside looking for his four-legged friend, but the dog wasn't around. Who would believe him if he shared what happened?

"A tree bit you?" they would scoff.

"No, a snake. The snake was part of the tree—part of the triple helix…" He couldn't even put it into words.

Every horrid thought entered his mind. He sat on the ground with a cloth covering his bleeding cheek. If they fired him for insanity, where would he go? Nobody needed a gardener because there were no gardens on the planet. Spending hours each day in a virtual world hooked up to a computer was a different kind of death—and not the way Kai wanted to spend the end of his days.

Maybe God, who created the plants, trees, and flowers that he so dearly loved, was punishing him for entertaining powerful people who claimed to be gods.

"Oh, God, please have mercy on me." But Kai heard nothing. He had never been a religious person anyway. Perhaps the Creator had gone to another universe to start over, but would a loving God abandon his creation? Surely he wasn't that fickle.

Besides, Kai wanted to preserve God's marvelous handiwork. Otherwise, the remnant he cherished would become extinct by a concoction that Frankenstein scientists dreamed up in a lab.

Unexpectedly, he felt the presence of something nearby. At first, he was terrified, but when Kai looked up, he saw the white dog standing beside him. Relieved, he reached over and wrapped his arm around his neck, clinging to him as if his life depended on it. Then the dog pulled away, ran a short distance, and arched back, wagging his tail.

"He's coaxing me to follow him," Kai said. He remembered the direction the dog was leading him—to the elderberries. He stood. The elderberries had healed the dog. Perhaps the berries could heal him.

He followed the dog, wondering how many elderberries he should eat, but after consuming a handful, he fell into a deep sleep. The following day, when he awoke, he was surprised he felt no lingering effects from the bite. He promised God as he began gardening, "there will be no triple helix plantings in this garden as long as I am the gardener." The question was, how could he destroy the tree that tried to kill him without getting caught?

An idea entered his mind. What was it, his boss said—expose the tree gradually to sunlight. What if he did it quickly? What if he burned the tree in the sunlight?

He wasted no time moving the triple helix to the brightest spot in the garden. He would also deprive the tree of nutrients and water.

Then he had another thought. He would hang a bright light over the tree at night after the sun went down. That way, the tree never saw darkness, and the third strand of the helix would have to endure unrelenting light. With no reprieve, the snake couldn't hide in the shadows, striking anything that came near. He was exposed now—a snake that wanted to substitute God's perfection with his counterfeit.

After a couple of weeks, the tree died, much to Kai's delight. He made careful readings of the tree's demise, and the snake disappeared into the tree, never to be seen again.

The scientists brought more trees, and they died, too, because of Kai's expertise. After a time, the scientists gave up and moved on to other projects. For now, the garden was safe under the care of Kai and the man's best friend. But who knew for how long?[1]

11

ENEMY OF THE SOUL

Jeremiah 9:21 (NKJV)

For death is come through our windows, has entered our palaces...

The aged woman drew the window blinds even tighter. "No light," she declared. "Light hurts my eyes. I mustn't let in the light."

She stuffed towels between the blinds and the glass window and taped the blinds to the windowsill. She lived alone, locked in self-imposed solitary confinement with little human contact. She wanted nothing—not love, not pity, not even comfort. Those emotions were for humans who still felt human, but she had become a fragment of humanness long ago. She didn't want to feel. She only lived to conquer the terror that welled up in her heart during the day and the predator that invaded her room at night.

"Why did they construct windows in this room?" she lamented. "I could keep 'it' out if it weren't for the windows."

Tap-tap-tap. The knocking on the door alerted her that her meal had arrived. She grabbed some cash from her cash jar and opened the door for the delivery man.

"Keep the change," she said, which was hardly a tip, but enough to keep him coming back the next day.

She wasn't going to eat immediately, but the smell of chicken and rice soon filled the room. She relented. Pulling up a chair, she sat beside the covered window—an obsession that filled her with dread, but her weak-willed spirit held her in bondage.

"I will conquer 'it' tonight," she mumbled. "I won't let 'it' into the room."

Night came earlier in the winter months, and soon shadows filled the room, etching strange patterns on the walls. She heard whispers through the window, the rattling of the blinds, and the lisping tree branches scraping the window. The screen had long ago been mutilated by "it."

"No," she cried out. "You can't come in." She tried to hold "it" back, the monster that wanted her. All night she fought it—with every ounce of physical and emotional strength she possessed. But "it" always won. She would fall asleep exhausted when "it" left at the first ray of sunlight. "It" hated the light—more than "it" hated her.

"If only I could be set free of my misery," she wrote on a piece of paper. "I don't want anything except to get rid of 'it.'"

Her husband had abandoned her, and her children had cut her off long ago. Somewhere on those streets below the window, they lived. "I must tame the window. I must keep 'it' out. I must conquer the enemy of my soul."

She didn't need love. She didn't need anything; she could take care of herself. If only she could destroy "it."

Then one day, she heard a different kind of knock. "Who could that be?" she muttered. Months had passed since anyone had come to see her. She timidly approached the door.

"Who is it?" she asked.

"I have a package for you, Ma'am," the voice said.

"A package?" she asked.

"Yes, Ma'am."

The woman unbolted the door, and a postman with a small brown envelope greeted her. "Can you sign here, Ma'am?"

The woman initialed the package receipt and closed the door. As she strolled toward the unkept bed, she read the name, "U.C. Little." Her heart skipped. She hadn't read that name in years—her ex-husband. Why would anyone be sending his package to her? She tore open the envelope to discover government papers inside.

Her ex-husband would need these papers, but she wouldn't send them to him. He should have taken care of this a long time ago. "Am I my ex-husband's keeper?" she asked.

She took great delight in tossing the papers aside. "Another chance for me to get back at him. He took away my dreams. He doesn't deserve anything from me."

That night, the darkness grew fiercer, and nightmares invaded her mind. The intensity of the spiritual attack made it difficult to tell the natural world from the unseen realm.

The following day, feeling tired and disheartened, she fixated her eyes on the covered window. "I can't keep 'it' out. I'm lost," and her defeatism brought her to her knees.

"It" is winning," she admitted. "I'm dying."

"If only...I could do things all over again." She turned to the table where the government documents lay discarded.

Weeks passed as she lamented her inability to defeat "it." With her strength diminishing, she was ready to give up. Living only to beat "it" was futile. She wanted to die, but that would mean "it" had conquered her. Never!

One morning, she heard a knock on the door. She recognized it as the knock she'd heard once before. "Another package?" she mused. "Surely not."

She went to the door, and the same postman stood there with another brown envelope.

"Can you sign here, Ma'am?"

The woman complied and shut the door. But this time, she didn't tear the package open and dump the contents on the table. Instead, she sat by the covered window with the envelope on her lap. Did she want to spend the rest of her life cut off from the world, her children, everything?

"What a waste," she heard a voice say. Startled, she glanced around the room, but no one was there.

She stood and walked to the dresser to pull out a pen and envelope. Where did her ex-husband live? She returned to the window chair and peeled back some tape from the blind. Eclipsed sunshine peeked through the open crack. Dull from darkness, her eyes flinched at the intense brightness.

What would U.C. Little think about the package when he received it? She attached a note—unthinkable a few weeks earlier.

She smiled, delighted that she could see the bright, unrelenting light. It didn't matter what U.C. Little thought—she could see the light.

12

THE GATEKEEPER

John 8:32 (NKJV)

And you shall know the truth, and the truth shall make you free.

Ivan, the gatekeeper, summoned the young lad, Leonid Portnoy. Having turned 21, Leonid was now considered an adult according to the village's laws. The majestic sun hung over Ivan's shoulder as he stood next to the gate. Gently rolling hills and pleasant valleys surrounded the obscure town. At an undisclosed location, it was the only city in the world where people didn't have to work if they didn't want to, and everything was provided to its residents for free.

Hidden City would remain hidden as long as Ivan was its gatekeeper. For decades, he had protected the village. As the oldest living resident, Ivan didn't know everyone in the town, but everyone without exception knew Ivan. And while his life was ending, he had never shared the secret to his longevity.

A stranger visited Ivan when he was young and told him some

truths that made him shudder. Ivan never saw the wanderer again, though he searched far and wide. Outsiders were not allowed in the village, so who he was remained a mystery. After all these years, Ivan never shared what the sage told him. Now, the sick man sat beside the gate with the setting sun at his back.

How many more days would he be able to perform his duties? He had summoned Leonid Portnoy to appear before him. Where was he? The perfumed flowers along the fence lifted his spirits. Ivan glanced at his watch and massaged his fingers to warm them. So much to say, Ivan mused, but so little time.

The hour was late, and Ivan admitted he had a sense of dread. Perhaps Leonid got off work late. Maybe he didn't see the summons. Life changed for all the young people in Hidden City when they turned 21. A house and car were awarded to each resident if he had been a good citizen. Money didn't exist. If a person wanted something, all he had to do was request it, and in 30 days, he received it—free of charge.

Many thought Hidden City was just folklore. But almost everyone who believed it existed wanted to live there. A few souls knew its location, but entry was forbidden under the death penalty.

By contrast, nobody from Hidden City ever wanted to leave. Why would they? Everyone was rich, could have whatever they wanted, and never went without food.

Ivan began to cough and reached into his robe pocket for a throat lozenge. He hoped to calm the cough before Leonid arrived when he would need to talk. The ongoing cough was a reminder of the progression of his disease. He would not escape the ravages of its curse despite outliving everyone else in Hidden City.

But at last, Ivan saw Leonid approaching.

"Sorry I'm late," Leonid said as he neared. "I stopped by the store on the way home. Only when I arrived did I see the summons."

Ivan waved his hand dismissively. "No problem, Leonid." Ivan pulled up a chair and pointed. "Please, have a seat. I have some business to discuss with you."

Leonid complied. "Am I in trouble?"

Ivan laughed. "Of course not. You are one of the most trusted young men, and..."

Relief crossed the lad's face that the gatekeeper wasn't going to reprimand him, but when Ivan stopped midsentence, Leonid leaned in. He didn't want to miss something important.

Ivan bit his lip, unsure of how much he should tell Leonid. There was no guarantee the young lad would agree to his business proposition; if he didn't, the information he shared could put Leonid at risk.

———

Leonid's life had not been easy. His parents died before he turned twelve, so he was raised by various families in the village. That was typical because most people died before age thirty. If someone lived to forty, that was unusual. Leonid didn't know how old Ivan was, but his white hair made him seem ancient. Ivan had no power beyond his duties as gatekeeper, but his old age earned him great respect.

Leonid's thoughts returned to the present. Why had Ivan summoned him out of the thousands who lived in the city? He anxiously waited for Ivan to finish his sentence. Soon the sun would set below the hills. Leonid did not like walking around after dark, especially when it was such a long journey back to his apartment.

"...and what?" Leonid asked.

Ivan glanced around, perhaps making sure no one could overhear their conversation.

"Leonid," Ivan said, "I want you to take over my duties as the gatekeeper of the village."

Leonid stared at Ivan in disbelief. To take over the duties of gatekeeper seemed way beyond his abilities. Not that it was hard, but the prestige that went with it, the trust of the government and the people—plus, it was a full-time job. Ivan's house was beside the gate. Did that mean he would live in Ivan's house? And what about Ivan? Did he not want to be the gatekeeper anymore?

"Why do you want to step down from being the gatekeeper?" Leonid asked. "It's the most prestigious job in the village."

Ivan's eyes appeared sad to Leonid. Perhaps Leonid didn't want to know the answer; he regretted asking the question.

But Ivan didn't wait this time to answer. "Leonid, I'm dying. I have the cough of death, and you are the only one I trust to take the job of gatekeeper."

He waved his hand. "I know the government will find someone to replace me if you don't accept my offer, but who knows if the appointed person might be dishonest. The outside world is very different. Money is needed to purchase things like food, cars, and housing. A greedy person who wanted to get rich could do so easily at the expense of the folks who live here and abscond with all that wealth outside the city gates."

"What's money?" Leonid asked. In Hidden City, everybody had plenty and needed nothing.

Ivan pointed to the barbwire fence. "Beyond that fence and gate, people live a long time. They don't die young. So supplies are limited, and there isn't enough food. The land is expensive. That's why everybody wants to come here. They know the residents can have everything they want. However, if the government allowed visitors into the village, Hidden City would be exposed for what it is, and the landowners don't want that to happen."

"Has anybody ever left Hidden City?" Leonid asked.

Ivan shook his head. "Anybody can leave, but they can never return."

"Why is that," Leonid asked. "I've never understood why."

Ivan lifted his head toward the heavens. "Leonid, there is a cost to freedom. In Hidden City, no one is free. And although everyone's life is shortened, the citizens have everything they need. Nobody goes without."

Leonid's heart focused on Ivan's words; everyone's life is shortened. "Why have you outlived everybody, Ivan? My parents died before they reached thirty."

"I can answer that only if you agree to be the gatekeeper," Ivan said.

Leonid stared across the fields outside the barbwire fence. What was out there? Leonid knew he only had two choices. He either left Hidden City forever or became the gatekeeper. He knew his conscience would bother him too much to turn down Ivan's offer and remain in the village.

The truth was Leonid had already contemplated leaving. He felt drawn to go—unlike his friends. Leonid knew the folks outside Hidden City lived longer. Once a week, supplies would arrive, and the delivery guys were often older—at least older than anybody in town. What would it be like to be free—but where would he get the money? That seemed important to the outside world, even though he didn't know what it was.

Leonid had often shared these thoughts with his friends and never understood why they were so disinterested. Why was he different? Finally, he replied, "Let me think about it for a day."

Ivan nodded. He reached inside his mantle and handed something to the lad. "I want to give you this book. Please keep it, but don't let anyone know you have it. It's forbidden in the village."

Leonid took the book from Ivan and examined it in the dim sunlight. "It's ancient, isn't it?"

Ivan nodded. "It belonged to the previous gatekeeper. He gave it to me before he died."

Ivan's words scared Leonid. "Suppose I decide that I want to leave the village? Is it forbidden"—Leonid pointed beyond the gate —"out there?"

"Only by those who hate the book," Ivan said. "But don't worry about that right now. Go home and read some of it. Then come back tomorrow, and we will talk some more."

Leonid bid his new mentor farewell. He had much to think about, and the book was thick. There was no way he could read it all in twenty-four hours.

When he returned home, his cooked dinner was waiting for him, and the aroma whetted his appetite; he had selected his meals the previous week. Tonight he had salmon—a rare delicacy in the village—with rice, asparagus, and cheesecake for dessert.

After finishing, he made himself comfortable in his favorite chair and pulled the book out of its protective covering. On the cover were the words *Holy Bible*.

"So this is a holy book," Leonid whispered. Holy books were not allowed in the village. He opened it and read the words handwritten on the first page: "True freedom is spiritual. John 8:32. 'And you shall know the truth, and the truth shall make you free.'"

For the next few hours, Leonid read the words in the holy book. He thought about what Ivan said, the barbwire fence surrounding Hidden City, and the gates that Ivan protected to keep outsiders from entering. As far as Leonid knew, nobody had ever left the city. Why couldn't they return if they did leave?

If freedom existed outside the barbwire fence, why would anyone want to come to Hidden City? Was it just curiosity?

But Leonid had one question the Bible didn't answer. Perhaps it didn't matter, but why did the residents of Hidden City die young and those beyond the barbwire fence live longer? And why had Ivan lived longer than everyone else?

That night Leonid tossed and turned in his sleep. For the first time, he felt an awakening. For years, questions had filled his mind about things that no one was allowed to talk about; could Ivan answer his questions? And if he did, would that make Leonid obligated to become the next gatekeeper?

Unexpectedly, the concept of freedom loomed large in Leonid's mind. New insights from the Bible and Ivan's words pricked his soul. Leonid remembered the Hidden City landowners telling the citizens they lived in paradise as special people. Was that the truth?

The lad turned on the lamp next to his bed and opened the book to re-read Ivan's handwritten words: "...and the truth shall make you free."

———

The next day at about the same time, Leonid returned to meet Ivan. Ivan appeared much older than the previous day, reminding Leonid that Ivan was sick. Leonid still didn't know what to do, but he didn't want to disappoint Ivan who had chosen him to take his position.

"Greetings," Leonid said.

"Thank you for returning," Ivan replied. "Did you have a chance to look at the book I gave you?"

Leonid nodded. "My eyes have been opened to things I never thought about before."

Ivan smiled. "The truth shall make you free. You can be free even here in Hidden City, where you are not free."

Leonid pointed beyond the gates, but before he could ask his question, he saw a man approaching. "Look."

Ivan stood to greet the outsider. "Can I help you?"

The man said, "I am a journalist, and I want to interview the gatekeeper of Hidden City."

"That's me," Ivan said, "but I don't do interviews. And you aren't allowed to videotape or take pictures. You can read it right there on the fence sign."

Ivan glanced at the fence where Leonid perceived a hidden camera.

"And I need to inform you, we are being watched," Ivan added.

The man said, "Thank you," and walked away.

Ivan said to Leonid, "Written in multiple languages, the fence sign says, 'No entry, no trespassing, no filming, and no photography.' That's why I am here, to ensure people follow the law."

Ivan began to cough, taking several minutes to get his voice back. "So what do you want to ask me, Leonid? My time is short, and I need to know tonight if you will take my position as gatekeeper. I may not live another twenty-four hours."

It took a moment for Leonid to recover after hearing this revelation. Dozens of questions swirled in his mind. Before his mentor died, Leonid needed to know the answer to one question that only Ivan could answer. "Ivan, why have you lived so long, and why does everyone else here die young?"

Ivan nodded. "Yes, I knew you would ask that. I shall tell you now as it weighs on me. Many years ago, spent nuclear waste was dumped here and contaminated the area. Certain parts of the village are more polluted than others. It depends on where you live and how much radiation exposure you receive as to when you will die. Those who receive the most radiation die first. Me—I never enter the village. I am the gatekeeper, and this is where I stay. I am at the rim of the exposure, on the border between where it's safe and where it's not. I've lived almost as long as those outside the village."

Leonid's eyes widened. "You mean we live on a nuclear waste site?"

Ivan's countenance fell. "Yes, that's what I mean."

"Why would anyone want to enter this wasteland?" Leonid asked. "That doesn't make sense. If the people of Hidden City don't know about the radiation, then they don't know to leave." Suddenly, Leonid felt like he wanted to get as far away as possible.

Ivan replied, "Leonid, there is a cost with freedom. Throughout history, many have died in the pursuit of freedom. But some people don't want freedom. They want to be taken care of by the government. They want possessions. They don't want to be productive citizens. Perhaps they are lazy; perhaps they are just unmotivated. But in return, unwittingly, they receive death. A famous American once said, 'Give me liberty, or give me death.'"

Leonid tried to comprehend everything Ivan told him, but his words were so packed with meaning that understanding them all at once was difficult.

"What about you, Ivan? You know all of this, yet you choose to be the gatekeeper. Why?"

"Do you remember the passage I quoted in the book?" Ivan asked.

Leonid nodded. "I memorized it. 'True freedom is spiritual. John

8:32 And you shall know the truth, and the truth shall make you free.'"

"You see, Leonid, I am free, even though I live between two very different worlds. The freedom I have comes from the words in that book, and no government or person can take that from me."

Leonid focused on Ivan's wisdom.

"My home is not here; I'm just a gatekeeper. Many people stop by—the curious, the simpleton, and the discerning—and I can share these truths. That is my calling. Because I protect the gate and do my job well, people trust me, and with age comes more respect. Most importantly, the truth in the book set me free so that I could share that truth with others. If you believe the words in the book, you will be free, too, no matter what you choose to do."

Ivan gazed into the heavens. "Soon, I must go to the place where eternal truth resides, and I will meet the gatekeeper who died to give me eternal freedom." Ivan paused. "Does that make sense?"

Leonid nodded. "And I bet they have no need for money in that place, do they?"

Ivan laughed. "You got it, Leonid. I knew that you would. There is no need for money. The debt to live there has already been paid."

"By Jesus?" Leonid asked.

"That's right," Ivan replied.

Leonid stood and walked over to the barbwire fence. He ran his fingers along the razor-thin edge of the wire. He noticed, perhaps for the first time, the rolling hills and wildflowers clinging to the rocks in the distance. Survival was difficult where freedom reigned.

Leonid turned toward his village, studying its kept pathways and modern structures. He contemplated his two futures. Then he faced Ivan with his decision. "My freedom comes from above. Let me take the mantle from you, and may I grow in wisdom to become as righteous as the gatekeeper who died for me."

Ivan smiled. "Bless you, Leonid. You will make an excellent gatekeeper."[1]

13

AND THEN THERE WAS ONE

2 Timothy 4:7 (NKJV)

"I have fought the good fight, I have finished the race,
I have kept the faith."

When Elan entered college, Friedrich Nietzsche was one of his heroes. In fact, at one time, Elan thought Nietzsche was a genius—until he read what he said about free will. Elan reached a crisis point as a philosophy student when he couldn't accept the beliefs of those he once admired. The 20-year-old believed that humans were free to make choices. He did not think that everything he accomplished in life was the result of some ethereal force that might be capricious or fickle.

"Free will must exist," Elan argued with his atheist friends, but where was that boundary between free will and pre-determinism?

When Elan heard Christians talking about free will, he thought they might know something that he didn't. The college student spent the next two years studying the Scriptures and became a Christian, to the shock of many. Not only did he confess Jesus as his Savior, but he was determined to go to graduate school and become a pastor or theologian.

One afternoon during his senior year, his pastor called him. "Elan," he said, "I received a letter in the mail addressed to you that says 'confidential' on the envelope."

"Who is it from?"

"There's no return address, but I don't think it's junk mail."

A pause ensued as Elan mentally checked off several names of friends who might have sent him something in jest, but he dismissed them. All of his friends texted when they wanted to communicate.

"I'll come to the church now," Elan said.

He made the ten-minute drive in only five. When he arrived, the secretary hurried him into the pastor's office.

Pastor Lehman was an older man close to retiring and had played an integral role in Elan's life following his conversion. After the perfunctory greetings, the pastor handed him the envelope. Elan opened it with a bit of sweat on his brow, but to his surprise, there was no writing on the stationery. As disappointment set in, he heard a voice inside his head.

"Elan, you have a dinner appointment this Friday at 6:00 p.m. at the Fountainhead Restaurant. Two messengers will greet you when you arrive. They will recognize you even if you don't know who they are. Will you be there?"

"Yes!"

"Yes—what?" Pastor Lehman asked.

For an instant, the college student forgot where he was. He stared at the blank invitation in his hand. Still somewhat shaken, he handed him the letter.

Pastor Lehman looked at it. "It's just a blank sheet of paper."

"I know," said Elan. "I heard a voice asking me if I could come to dinner at the Fountainhead Restaurant Friday at 6:00 p.m. The voice said two messengers would greet me even though I may not know them. I said I would be there."

———

Friday arrived, and at the appointed time, Elan, dressed in his Sunday best, walked up the sidewalk to the Fountainhead Restaurant. Two men in white robes appeared at the entrance, and Elan, with his heart pounding and more than a drop of perspiration on his forehead, shook their hands.

The messengers, whether angelic or human, Elan wasn't sure, ushered him inside. The sweet aroma of fresh bread filled his nostrils, and the beaded sweat on his forehead evaporated in the coolness of the air. Hues of various intensities filtered through the restaurant, radiating beauty like exquisite gems, and the view through the windows reflected nothing he had ever seen. The restaurant seemed to be floating in the clouds.

One messenger escorted Elan to a table where three other young men sat. Each one introduced himself by his first name, Bill, David, and John. Elan took a seat beside them and engaged them in conversation. "Are you guys from around here?"

"Where is here?" Bill asked.

Elan chuckled. "That's a good question."

Hungry folks filled the restaurant, some older, some younger, and some—well, they seemed ageless. As the young men talked, Elan learned they were also college students and new Christian converts. None lived near him in Florida. Bill was from California, David was from Texas, and John lived in Rhode Island.

Soon a waiter brought them water and bread, and they engaged in conversation about their goals. Like Elan, they were driven to achieve great things for Christ. After a while, when Elan looked at his watch, he couldn't believe an hour had passed.

At that moment, one of the messengers reappeared, and his mysterious words prompted more unanswered questions.

"You have just eaten manna from heaven and tasted living water. When you leave, do many good works. If you remain faithful— perhaps many years from now—you'll meet again for the second course."

"Good works?" Elan asked. "You mean—like in a Christian sense?"

The messenger nodded. "Good works are what you do—feeding

the poor, sharing the Good News, serving in church, teaching the Bible—all those things you long to do in your heart now. The devil wants to steal your hunger for the Lord. Only three of you will return for the second course."

The college students exchanged glances. Elan felt a lump in his throat. Would he return? Or would he succumb to the world's temptations or be led astray?

———

Elan finished college and went to seminary. While in seminary, he fell in love with the school librarian, and the couple married when Elan graduated. A small church hired him, and he was an associate pastor for the next two years.

Late one night, when Elan was praying, he remembered the restaurant encounter with the two messengers. What were the other three men up to—had they been faithful in good works? So much time had passed, Elan lamented his unworthiness in God's sight, that he had not been invited back for the second course.

As he prayed and sought forgiveness, he heard a messenger's voice.

"Elan, do you hear me?"

"Here I am." He looked around but saw no one in his study. Even the dog was asleep.

"Go to the Fountainhead Restaurant Friday at 6:00 p.m., and I will meet you there."

Elan thought about how far away the restaurant was from his home now. How could he even get there since he and his wife shared one car? But before he could reply, the voice spoke,

"Elan, there is a Fountainhead Restaurant in this small town."

"I'll be there," Elan said, and his spirit soared. The week went by slowly. He had never shared with anyone about the previous encounter, but now he would.

His wife just smiled when Elan told her. After kissing him, she said, "You never told me you had entertained angels. Just don't wait this time to tell me what happens."

Elation filled Elan's heart. Thankfully his wife didn't think he was hallucinating. He spent the next few days in prayer, reading his Bible, and fasting. Friday night couldn't come soon enough.

———

Much to Elan's surprise, he found the Fountainhead Restaurant through an internet search, and Friday night, he arrived at the restaurant clean-shaven and wearing his Sunday best. He had even been to the barber, which greatly pleased his wife. He arrived an hour early, perhaps over-exuberant to meet the messengers. When they weren't there, doubt crept in. Suppose he was hallucinating that night? After all, at that very moment when he heard the voice, he was lamenting not being invited back, blaming it on his many failures and doubting his worthiness.

Before he could get too gloomy, Bill and David arrived—thirty minutes early. Did that mean John was the one who would not return?

Bill and David were all smiles, and the three young disciples of Christ exchanged handshakes and slapped each other on the back.

"Great to see you, Elan," Bill and David said, with the unspoken acknowledgment that John would not join them.

As they were talking, two messengers in shining robes appeared. "Good evening, Gentlemen." They escorted the young men into the restaurant and took them to a window table.

"This special table is reserved for you," the server said.

Once again, the view was breathtaking. The vibrant colors of the clouds were heavenly, creating a kaleidoscope of images beyond human experience.

The restaurant was half full, unlike last time when it was so crowded. Elan imagined what the second course might be.

Sweet aromas filled the restaurant with delicacies he couldn't wait to taste. The three men shared their lives over the past decade. They had all become pastors, and two were shepherding churches. Bill was a missionary to an unreached people group in Africa.

Soon the second course arrived, and four plates of steaming hot food filled the serving tray. Who was the fourth plate for since there were only three of them?

The messenger answered Elan's thought. "Take what you want. John's talents will now go to the three of you."

The men dove into the food. Elan couldn't remember when he had tasted such heavenly salmon. God knew his favorite entrée and fed him precisely what he would have ordered under ordinary circumstances.

When they finished, one of the messengers returned, thoughtfully gazing at the men. "The next course will be the dessert, but only two of you will be invited back."

Who would not return? Elan wondered.

The messenger added, "Remember, your good works are not for salvation but rewards."

"What happened to John?" Elan asked. "Did he lose his salvation?"

The messenger replied. "No, you can't lose your salvation. However, if you fall away because of sin, you lose rewards. The rewards you would have earned are forfeited, and God gives the talents for those rewards to others."

Elan returned home, thinking about John. He had seemed so full of the Holy Spirit; he could quote Scripture better than all of them. What happened?

Many years went by. Elan served in several pastoral roles, but life was not easy in the pulpit or at home. One trial after another came his way, almost to the point he wanted to quit the pastorate.

But his wife encouraged him. "Don't give up," she would say. "If you are faithful, God will reward you."

He tried to be a good father but felt he often failed. As he grew in the knowledge of the Lord, he often doubted that God would call him worthy of anything. Sin always seemed crouching at the door, tempting him to do wrong things. How easy it would have been to have an affair, steal money from the church, or teach only from his favorite Scriptures without digging deep and teaching from the entire Bible.

Then one night, a voice awakened him in a dream. "Elan."

Elan recognized the voice and sat up in bed.

"Meet me at the Fountainhead Restaurant this Friday at 6:00 p.m."

The family had moved two times since the previous engagement, but Elan knew there must be a Fountainhead Restaurant in the small town somewhere.

"I'll be there," Elan said. He was so excited he could hardly go back to sleep. He thought about waking up his wife to tell her, but she lay so peacefully beside him that he decided to wait until the morning.

———

6:00 p.m. Friday arrived, and Elan showed up an hour early. His wife had taken him shopping for a new suit—which he had put off buying for years, and he had made a trip to the barber. Why? Elan wasn't sure because he was almost bald.

He saw that Bill was waiting, and his old friend greeted him warmly. "It's so good to see you, Elan."

Elan chuckled. "I guess it's just you and me for the dessert."

Bill glanced around, looking for the messengers.

Elan noted how much older Bill looked. Thirty years had passed since their first encounter when they were still college students. Maybe David had died. He had seemed so full of the spirit, so driven to serve God. Surely, he was still doing so. Of the four of them, Elan figured he would be the one to finish strong. But David wasn't here for dessert. That meant only the two of them had a chance to end well.

The two messengers appeared, and they again escorted them inside the restaurant. The room was almost empty, with just a few patrons eating. As before, the view was spectacular. They floated in the clouds with the stars like messengers singing songs of praise.

The two men talked about their lives, families, and careers. Soon one of the messengers arrived with four dessert plates—including Elan's favorite, chocolate cheesecake. The angel said, "The other two men who started with you have lost their rewards, so their talents have been passed on to you. Use them for the glory of God; at the last course, you will understand."

"If this is dessert," Elan asked, "what is the last course?"

The messenger replied. "Remember, the Bible says, 'Taste and see the goodness of the Lord.' Now you taste; next time, you will see."

Elan felt sad only one of them would make it. Emboldened, he asked the obvious. "Can we not both finish strong?"

The angel studied Elan, peering into his eyes with so much love Elan's heart melted. "You each have free will," the messenger replied. "You can receive all the rewards God wants to give you, but the reality is, one of you will finish well, and one of you won't. Jesus has given you salvation, but you must earn rewards."

Elan thought back to his first two years in college when he embraced an atheistic theology and admired men like Nietzsche. How good God had been to rescue him. Later that evening, Elan prayed, "Please, Jesus, help me to finish well."

———

Years passed. Elan's two sons grew up, married, and he became a grandfather. Then his wife died, and the joy of living left him. He was old now, and the tasks of daily living were challenging. He limped, his eyes were dim, and he could no longer hear the birds singing.

"Perhaps the angel spoke to me, and I didn't hear," Elan lamented. Nevertheless, he continued to live for God's glory, more determined than ever to finish well. He no longer cared about rewards, whether he earned one or none. He only longed to see Jesus.

Despite being weak and frail, Elan read his Bible daily and prayed. When the day came that he breathed his last, his sons were by his side. He knew this was his departure to glory, and he had never shared with them his religious experience. And so he shared the story with his sons.

"I guess I wasn't found worthy," Elan said. "I never heard from the messenger again. Even though I won't receive any rewards, I'm okay with that. All I want is Jesus."

His older son, whose heart was tender, replied, "The last course is the real thing, Dad. Now you will 'see' the goodness of the Lord."

Elan thought about that. Maybe his son was right, and he tried to remember the messenger's final words.

———

The day of glory came, and two angels escorted Elan to his heavenly Father's house. An unfathomable number of people filled the celestial city. As the angels led the new arrival through the eternal gates, he saw his college friend, John, way back in the sea of people.

Elan reflected on the angel's words. John was in heaven because Jesus paid the price for his sins. Salvation was God's gift, but one must earn rewards. John would never be close to Jesus because he had forfeited his talents.

The messenger escorted Elan through the heavenly city, and he passed David and Bill along the way. The blessed abode would have blinded him without spiritual eyes to see even as God's unconditional love filled his reborn spirit. The freshness of heaven's rarified air and the angelic voices praising the Father were just glimpses of perfection. So much more awaited discovery. Oh, the magnitude of what he would have missed if it weren't for Jesus' death on the cross and his triumphant resurrection. When Elan neared the last course, he saw his risen Savior. Overcome with emotion, he worshiped.

The King of Kings walked over to Elan and welcomed him. "Well done, my good and faithful servant."[1]

14

NO FEAR

Isaiah 35:4 (NKJV)

Say to those who are fearful-hearted, "Be strong, do not fear! Behold, your God will come with vengeance, with the recompense of God; He will come and save you."

The cemetery beckoned Deborah's mother every year about this time, but Deborah didn't know why. She suspected, but her mother wouldn't tell her.

"It's enough that you know your nanny rests in peace here," is all she would say, "until the right time comes to tell you."

Deborah reminisced. Her beloved grandmother was so intelligent, so beautiful, and so kind. She wouldn't have hurt a fly.

Even in the noonday sun, the weather was cold, and Deborah wondered why they couldn't come to the cemetery in the summer when it was warmer. Her mother placed some flowers beside the headstone, and as she leaned over, Deborah could see tears in her reddened eyes.

Deborah's memories of her grandmother were dreamlike because she was so young when her grandmother disappeared, but she remembered vividly the last time she saw her Nanny. It was her favorite memory from childhood.

"Mother, what happened to Grandma?"

The older woman remained silent. Deborah sensed her mother

wanted to tell her, but she couldn't. Every time she tried, she choked up, and the words wouldn't come out.

Deborah propped up the red flowers and ran her fingers over the dates on the stone marker. She longed for one last conversation with Nanny. Death was so final, especially for one so young. The date on the tombstone was only a few weeks after that momentous event in Washington, D.C. Deborah remembered her grandma that day as healthy and vibrant, laughing and singing as she pushed Deborah in the stroller.

Now fourteen and a young woman, she believed she could handle the secret her mother hid in her heart. She was old enough to think about serious things and determined not to let another year pass without knowing the truth.

She turned to her mother sitting beside her, but at that moment, the stricken woman bent over and turned away. The young girl lovingly touched her mother's shoulder. "The last time I remember seeing Nanny was when we went to Washington, D.C."

Deborah's mother faced her daughter, and the old woman held her pointed index finger to her lips. "You mustn't talk about that day. The drones hide in secret places," and she sternly admonished Deborah a second time, her words clipped with fear.

But Deborah didn't care who heard. She wanted to speak her heart. "That day was my favorite day as a child. You, grandma, and I were together. I don't know where pappa was, but the three of us were there, and I remember the music, the beautiful singing, and everybody praying."

Deborah stopped speaking as if a new revelation gripped her. "Mother, we never hear beautiful music anymore."

Resignation crossed her mother's face. "You mustn't ever talk about that day again, you hear me, Honey?"

The fragile moment beguiled Deborah. Discouraged but unwilling to admit she had been cheated of the truth once more, she would try again later. The two returned to their tiny one-room house that looked like every other house on the street. The houses were so close together everyone knew everybody else's business.

Several times each day, drones scoured the sky looking into windows for something, although nobody knew what. Sameness was important. Nobody wanted to stand out. Nobody wanted to be recognized. Nobody wanted to be seen or heard.

Deborah remembered her grandmother loved to read. She remembered the books that lined the walls of her living room and bedroom. Nanny was the most intelligent person she knew, yet somebody took her away. How could someone so amazing disappear?

Nanny never did anything wrong. Why wouldn't her mother tell her? Deborah had even scoured the Internet, hoping to find her grandmother's name. But it was like she never existed.

January 6, 2021, was only eleven years ago, yet there were only a few articles about that day on the Internet. How could there be so few references when Deborah remembered the hundreds of thousands, perhaps millions, of people walking beside her in the stroller?

Deborah knew what the government said—many people had died that day, all at the hands of "Trump supporters and right-wing religious fanatics" who took over the Capitol. Because of the widespread destruction and damage, the government hauled many off to jail.

Was her beloved Nanny one of those eyewitnesses arrested? How could that be when Nanny wouldn't even kill a spider?

Besides, they wouldn't have gone to the event if there was any danger. Nanny was an American patriot and wanted to be there that day. How could Deborah learn what happened? Did her mother even know? Or had she been brainwashed to forget? Deborah knew those things happened routinely. It was called re-education.

As Deborah watched her mother twist and turn in bed, uttering groanings too deep to understand, the young girl went through everything she could remember on January 6, 2021, and the days and weeks that followed.

It wasn't long after that that her dad went off to war. According to government reports, he was a hero, but Deborah didn't believe those reports. Why didn't he ever come home? The government said America was winning the war, but how could anyone know? No one knew what happened outside the country. She hadn't seen her father in years, but occasionally, her mother would receive a letter declaring he had won another medal for his heroism.

Deborah didn't care about medals. Her mother would scold her, "You have food to eat, a roof over your head, and clothes to wear. What more do you want?" And then, emotionally spent, her mother would stomp off.

Deborah felt sorry for her mother. At least Deborah was honest with her feelings; her mother just believed her own lies. But she could never come up with a good answer to her mother's questions. Yes, they had food, clothes, and a roof, but Deborah felt like a person with no future. Is this how she wanted to live the rest of her life?

The two-week winter break would end soon, and Deborah would have to return to school. But the nightmares were unrelenting and made it difficult for her to focus on academics. She would see herself in the stroller among the thousands on that wide road, swept up in the music, the celebration, and the enchantment of the day's festivities. And then everything went dark. Two of the dearest people in her life disappeared.

What happened? None of what the state-run media said was as she remembered. But she was only a young child that day; maybe she was too young to remember.

Deborah walked over to her mother as she rested on their small bed. Mother probably wished she would turn out the lights so she could sleep. But Deborah was determined to find out what happened.

"Mother," Deborah asked, "do we have any books from Nanny's old house?"

Mother sighed. "Even if I had any, I wouldn't show them to you. You know books have been banned unless they are state-approved."

"So her books are not state-approved?"

"I didn't say that," her mother quipped.

"Why can't I know what happened to my grandmother? Why?"

Her mother sat up in bed and glared at Deborah. "Your grandmother was a domestic terrorist. She was sent off to prison and died. What more do you want to know?"

Deborah didn't like her mother's rebuff. "Don't you care about my feelings? I loved Grandma, domestic terrorist or not."

"I don't want to talk about it anymore," her mother scoffed.

Deborah glared at her. "You don't really believe that, do you? Nanny was so smart, compassionate, and—she loved Jesus."

Mother's eyes moistened. "Don't say that name, or they will come and take you to a re-education camp."

Deborah retorted. "Some things are more important. You've allowed the government to take over your mind. Fear is your constant companion. Nanny would never let that happen."

Mother leaned into Deborah and whispered. "And that's why they transported her to a re-education camp." Mother's countenance fell. "I've lost everyone important to me. I'd die if something happened to you."

"Please, Mother," Deborah insisted, "just show me one book of hers. Just one. I can hold the book to my chest and feel Nanny's presence in my heart."

Her mother glanced around the small house and whispered, "Unplug everything, the computer, TV—better yet, cover them up with towels. Close the blinds. And we must do it quickly before the nightly drone stops by and hovers in front of the window.

Quickly they concealed anything that could send or receive information, and Deborah followed her mother as she walked over to a small closet in the corner of the room. The older woman slid the door aside, knelt to move some boxes, and then stacked them on top of each other. Where the boxes had been, several loose tiles appeared.

A small hole emerged. Deborah gasped. "I never knew there was anything underneath the tiles."

Her mother retrieved two books—a family album and a Bible. "At least I have these. Our social score would drop to zero if they discovered them in my possession. You wouldn't be able to go to college. They would force us to live on starvation rations."

She handed Deborah the book with photographs.

Deborah opened the photo album and saw pictures of when she was little, along with her pappa and mom. Her mother was so beautiful, and her grandmother was stunning. Deborah sat back and cherished the family memories. She gently touched a photograph of her father and grandmother. She whispered under her breath, "What happened to them?"

Deborah continued to pore over more photos, noticing something she didn't expect to see—wealth. Nanny's house was huge.

Unexpectedly, Deborah remembered things she had forgotten. Like her grandmother playing the piano, the rides they took in Nanny's car to the park, and the ice cream store they would visit on the way home. What happened to that world? When had she last tasted ice cream?

Sadness overcame Deborah. She set the family album aside. What had started as an exciting adventure into the past became an overwhelming lump of sorrow in her throat.

"Can I see Nanny's Bible?" Deborah asked.

Her mother handed the old book to her, and Deborah ran her fingers along the frayed edges. Had she seen one of these before? Deborah closed her eyes—and remembered. "Where is that book you used to read to me that had Bible stories?"

Mother shook her head. "My only two books are Nanny's Bible and these family photos." Her voice quivered. "Deborah, only a tiny bit longer. It's getting late, and the drone will be coming by at any moment."

Deborah blurted out, "What good is it if you don't read the Bible? Or even look at these photographs? How can you enjoy them hidden in a dark closet?"

"They're so precious, Deborah. I don't want to risk losing them. They would take these from me if they knew I had them. Or worse."

Deborah opened the Bible and found a note inside.

"Oh, the note," Mother exclaimed, "I forgot about the note. Please read it."

Deborah whispered the words to her mother. "Dear Deborah, God told me someday you would find this Bible. The demons will flee if you call on the name of Jesus. Seek the truth, and never give up. Love, Nanny."

Deborah swallowed hard and handed the note to her mother. "Mother, something supernatural happened on January 6, 2021, which changed America. Why didn't the people who were there speak up? Why didn't they tell the truth? Why did they let the news media spread lies?"

Deborah's mother lowered her eyes. "Because if they did, they would have been arrested, like your dear Nanny. She spoke the truth. She knew what the CCP had done in China. That's why she took extra pamphlets to share with others. Nobody thought the CCP would take over America, except perhaps a few conspiracy lunatics."

Deborah thought about the CCP pamphlets her mother and grandmother handed her that day. She remembered circling the letters "CCP" etched in bold letters on the covers. Of course, as a child, they were just letters—nothing significant or earth-shattering. But because Nanny had handed them to her to hold, she felt important. Never could she have imagined the dire warnings in those words. If only America had taken those warnings seriously.

Deborah grabbed her mother's hand. "They were warning the people, weren't they? They knew what was coming, those people in the booths."

Mother nodded. "We must put these books back and open the blinds," Mother said. "We can't wait any longer. It's late."

Deborah wrapped her arms around the Bible and imagined she could smell the faint scent of her dear Nanny. She breathed in deeply. "I want to sleep with Nanny's Bible."

"If they see you with that …" her mother's voice trailed off.

"It's the Bible, Mother. They will not see it. God will protect us."

Mother bit her lip and hesitated, and for the first time in years, Deborah saw hope in her eyes.

"I believe you," her mother said. "I want to trust God. If only I had more faith."

Deborah and her mother clasped each other tightly. Then Deborah released her hold and said, "I remember something Nanny once said, 'Joy comes in the morning.'"

Her mother nodded.

"No fear," Deborah said. "No fear."[1]

15

DOOR NUMBER 1

Isaiah 45:7 (NKJV)

"I form the light and create darkness, I make peace
and create calamity; I, the Lord, do all these
things."

I stood in the foyer and stared at Door Number 1. The only choice I had was the order of the doors. So I could know the future to warn others—wasn't that what the voice said?

I turned the handle. The door opened to a room of mirrors. However, these weren't regular mirrors; they were mirrored doorways. "Which one should I enter, Lord?"

I heard nothing. I waited a little longer, but God's voice was silent. He left the choice to me; I wanted to choose wisely. I stepped around several and came to a tall mirror. I stuck my hand in and pulled it out. I passed up that one and several others until I came to a mirror with moving images. I entered that one.

I was in a world of moving sidewalks. They went to the north, south, east, and west, crisscrossing each other, intersecting, and moving at very high speeds.

I looked at my feet and stood on the word "Go" in a multi-dimensional space. As I studied the moving tele-transports, I noticed travelers. Some of the people were anxious. Others seemed to enjoy the journey. Some disappeared and reappeared farther down the road. Others popped up and stayed.

I watched, mesmerized. I tried to see people's faces. Who was happy and who was sad? That wasn't made clear to me.

There were more than a dozen sidewalks. The longer I mulled over which one to choose, the more uncertain I became. After a while, I grew weary. I threw up my hands. Choices carry eternal consequences, and I wanted to make the right one.

"You choose," I heard a voice say. "Free will is a wonderful thing in the hands of an awesome God."

The sidewalk whisked me alongside dozens of other travelers. As the moving sidewalk carried me, I saw foods that whet my appetite. Cinnamon rolls, chocolate croissants, and other pastries called my name. I passed a brewery with a sign advertising free samples of beer. Farther along, I caught a whiff of delightful scents —perfumes, essential oils, and soaps—so many choices, so much opportunity.

The exchange of money increased. Soon I saw people buying things they couldn't afford. They pulled out credit cards, signed bank loans, borrowed from friends, and more.

"I've maxed out my credit cards," someone said.

"No problem," a merchant replied. "Just sign here."

I left that conversation and continued along the widening sidewalk of debt.

"This car will be the best you've ever owned," a salesman exhorted. "It's the number one rated sports car in the world."

I looked at the price tag—a hundred thousand dollars.

Soon I came to a crosswalk. Until now, I didn't know the sidewalks were named. To my surprise, I was traveling on the Sidewalk of Necessities. I came to a store where a merchant was selling animals. The buyer offered the seller money, which was no small amount.

The merchant shook his head. "That's not enough. These animals are extinct. You can breed them and create a new Garden of Eden. Imagine the people who will flock to your attraction—people who love Mother Earth, conservationists, animal lovers, and bird enthusiasts. You'll be the richest man in the world. Who wouldn't want to visit the rebirth of the Garden of Eden?"

The bartering continued. What would be a fair price to buy extinct animals and create another Garden of Eden?

As I walked, I came to a merchant who was selling futures. "Hear ye," he shouted as he waved his hand. "Step right up. We'll release your heartfelt dream. It's reasonably priced, and you deserve it. Come and see a demonstration of the only dream reaper in the world."

A woman walked up. "What's the price?"

The wiry man whipped out his hand and pointed with a dramatic flair. "Have a seat. If you qualify after this demonstration, you'll be given a special seat in the real dream reaper." I looked behind the salesman at a most unusual contraption.

The woman was in her late twenties or early thirties and appeared to be in good health. Youth was leaving her, as it does for all of us, but she was too immature to have attained wisdom.

The woman poured out her heart to the stranger in extraordinary detail, expounding on all the unfair and unjust things that had happened to her, leading to a life in the gutter of despair. Always the victim, she wallowed in self-pity and rejection.

The merchant smiled. "You're just the right person for the dream reaper. You deserve better. Don't worry about the cost. You can pay it off in the next thirty years before your date with death."

"What do you mean, my date with death?"

The merchant replied, "Well, I can't tell you more than that. You'll need to talk to the dream reaper. He can answer that question."

She looked around. "Where is he?"

The merchant pointed. "Step right up to the dream reaper building."

The woman hesitated.

"You want to release your dream, right?"

The woman nodded, but her enthusiasm dissipated when she

realized she couldn't have it—another unjust and unfair thing to add to her trophy list of unhappiness.

I continued walking. A merchant stood out front waving a strange-looking banner—Soul Extractor. No one was at his stand, so I left the Sidewalk of Necessities and strolled over to the merchant.

"Tell me about your soul extractor business."

His eyes lit up, and he greeted me with such exuberance I felt indebted to make a purchase.

"Would you like your soul extracted?" the man asked me.

"What do you do with the soul once you extract it?"

"Oh," the merchant said, "I give it to the devil."

"What do you mean?"

"Have you ever met a person without a soul?"

"Wait a minute," I interrupted. "If I sell my soul to you, then I no longer have a soul."

"That's right," the merchant said. "But for some people, other things are more important than their soul."

I stared at the merchant.

The man leaned over and peered into my eyes. "Think about it," he whispered.

"You mean people would sell their souls?"

He sneered. "Absolutely."

"What do you give them for their soul?"

The man cocked his head as if surprised by my question. "The devil sets the price."

So what do you do with the soul you extract?"

The man laughed. "As I said, I give it to the devil."

"You can't do that," I protested.

The smile left his face. "Look, I'm not discussing the moral issue of it. All I care about is selling the soul, and all the devil cares about is receiving the soul. So we have the soul extractor. Everyone is happy. The person has what he wanted, I've made the transaction, and the devil has the soul."

I shook my head. "How can you do that?"

He leaned over and whispered, "Because I sold my soul to the devil, and now I do his bidding. I have no choice. He owns me."[1]

16

WHERE I COME FROM

Romans 1:18 (NKJV)

For the wrath of God is revealed from heaven against
all ungodliness and unrighteousness of men, who
suppress the truth in unrighteousness...

"Where I come from, men are boys, and women are girls," Frank said to his college-age son.

Dane slumped back in the living room chair. He glanced over at his mother, her eyes wet with tears. What could he say to ease the suffering of his parents upon learning that he was gay?

"Will you still love me?" Dane asked. "Or will you ostracize me like some Christian parents do when their children embrace a different lifestyle?"

His father and mother exchanged glances.

"We will always love you," his mother replied, "but this is hard for us to accept."

Dane's father added, "What's more concerning to us is you have rejected Jesus as your Lord and Savior."

The son's defenses shot up, and his face turned beet red. He did not want to hear anything about Jesus. He'd listened to enough Christians blast gays and lesbians and others like him. He could not embrace a God who would send people to hell. What kind of a God would do that?

"Dad, if you love me, you will accept me as I am. If God is love—I mean, he made me this way, and I know he loves me. If your love is real, then I hope you will, too. Otherwise, what good is Christianity if it permits you to hate certain groups of people? Isn't that hypocritical?"

Not able to handle any more of the conversation, Dane's mother got up and left the room. Dane winced. He knew this wouldn't be easy for them, but it was more painful than he imagined. He had projected unspoken messages about his gayness, but they didn't pick up on the cues. Or perhaps it was easier to ignore the subtle hints.

Father and son painfully eyed each other, a bond close to breaking. Dane was their only child, and if they had dreams of becoming grandparents, he had stripped them of that—and probably other aspirations that he would never know. Those hopes would be nothing more than fantasies buried deep in their psyche.

He had hidden behind a "straight" façade for too long, pretending to be a man when he felt like a woman. All his close friends were women. He didn't relate to men in the way other guys did. Could his father accept him the way he was? Dane expected they'd come around eventually and understand his world.

He stood to leave. "I guess I'll head back to the dorm." He couldn't think of anything else to say to comfort his parents except to give them time to accept that their only child was gay.

Dane's father walked him to the door. Placing his hand on his son's shoulder, he said, "It's not that you're gay that upsets me the most. You've rejected Jesus, and only Jesus can heal you."

Dane knew he wouldn't win this argument. To bring the conversation to a close, he said, "If God is real, pray that he will reveal himself to me in a way that's so supernatural that I can't deny he's talking to me."

Frank replied, "Okay."

Dane scoffed. "That will be the day," and he started to leave.

"Wait." His father uttered a quick prayer at the door. "Dear Father, please honor Dane's request. In Jesus' name."

Dane laughed uneasily. "Well, you didn't have to take me literally, but that's fine." He slipped out of his dad's embrace and headed down the front steps. "Tell Mom I love her."

"I will," Frank said. "Drive safely. And remember, there's power in the name of Jesus."

The boy got into his car and turned on the ignition. He slowly backed out of the driveway and sped off—but his destination was not what he anticipated.

———

Dane reached over and pressed the console button to turn on the DVD, but nothing happened. It was dark, and he didn't want to attempt to figure it out while driving, so he switched to the radio, but all he heard was static. "Odd." He ran a quick scan—nothing. He didn't see the option to connect to his phone. He must have disconnected the blue tooth.

Irritated, he focused on the road—it was only a few minutes to the dorm anyway. He pulled onto a dark two-lane alley that served as a cut-through when he was in a hurry. Why did the street seem so dark tonight?

Unexpectedly, the car slipped into neutral. The engine quit, and he had no power. When the car's forward momentum stopped, he found himself sitting in the middle of the road. He looked out the window. Why was it so dang dark? An EMP attack went through his head; is this what one would be like if it happened?

He reached into his back pocket to pull out his phone, but it wasn't there. He remembered reading a text message at his parent's house and laying the phone on the table. No wonder the blue tooth didn't connect. He would have to return because he needed his phone for school.

He attempted to restart his car but to no avail. Panic formed as he sat in the middle of the dark road. Even the emergency flashers didn't work.

He opened the door and stepped onto the street. He had no flashlight, no headlights, and no phone. He wasn't even sure where he was. He had taken this shortcut dozens of times but didn't see any houses to clue him in. Was it just dark, or was something else going on?

He had emergency road service but needed a phone to call for help. After locking the car, he started walking. The road would have little traffic at this late hour, so hopefully, no one would ram his vehicle.

He must have walked a mile when he came to a house with an inside light burning. As he approached, he hesitated. It appeared to be the house that was open on Halloween every year—the famous haunted house. People came from miles around to experience the haunted house extravaganza. He didn't think anyone occupied it, but the light inside indicated otherwise.

Dane had never been to the extravaganza—too spooky for him. While he didn't believe in Jesus, neither did he mess around in the occult. No drugs, no boos, no pornography—well, maybe just a tiny bit to satisfy his curiosity, but according to the holy book, Dane considered himself a pretty decent guy. He saw no reason to engage in the "cult of Jesus." He was a good person. According to his parent's definition, he was at odds with God's holy book, but his parents were wrong.

Dane referenced numerous Scriptures in the Bible to support his position that Jesus loved everybody. A God of love would never send anybody to hell. So he took great care not to think about that place. Despite his parents' concerns, God would not send him there.

His father said where he came from, men were boys and women were girls, but the Bible didn't say that. How old fashion his parents were.

Dane's thoughts returned to the present. Should he approach the haunted house? Perhaps a family lived there now. Why keep walking if someone could help him? He just needed to borrow a phone.

He crept up to the house quietly as the darkness whispered to him. Leaves rustled in the wind, and tree branches scraped against the eaves. He imagined a bat or some night creature lunging at him, and he hurried to reach the front porch. He knocked. Nobody answered. So he knocked again—nothing.

He glanced through the window, and the light was still burning. Someone must be inside. Curious, he turned the door handle. To his surprise, the door was unlocked. He pushed it forward and poked his head in to see. The light emanated from an adjacent room—the only light for miles. Darkness enveloped the rest of the house. Suppose someone was in there holding a gun. He was breaking into someone's home.

"Hello," Dane shouted. "Anyone here?"

Nobody appeared. "How could someone not hear me?" Dane bemoaned.

Gathering all the courage he could muster, he tiptoed through the dark entryway into what he perceived to be the living room. He would have to go around the corner to reach the lit room. When he eased around the protruding wall, he saw the light. Aghast, a burning flame swept toward him, and the blaze pulled him into a dark, swirling vortex hidden in the fire. He descended into unending nothingness.

———

Dane hated the feeling of falling, and he screamed at the top of his lungs. His voice reverberated off walls that sounded like he was in a tunnel. With eyes clenched, his life passed before him—the good, the bad, and the ugly. Convinced he would die, he was shocked to see how much of his life was sinful. Now it was too late to do anything about it.

Amazingly, he didn't die when he landed, and while the fall didn't kill him, he feared a heart attack might. He could hardly catch his breath as he lay on the damp, cavernous bottom,

Dane leaned over and vomited. What he wouldn't give for water in the intense heat. Exhausted, he pulled himself up to his feet, and as his eyes adjusted, he saw fires burning. The screams of desperate voices filled his ears, and an overwhelming sulfuric smell made him nauseous again.

"Get me out of here," a voice cried.

Somebody must have heard something. He wasn't about to rescue anyone. He wanted to get away, but how could he? Looking ahead and glancing behind and even above him, everything reflected in multiple directions, as if a prism had trapped him in legions of dimensions.

Despite his reluctance, he edged closer to the fire, and overwhelming heat scorched his skin. Vaguely he could make out images of bodies in the flickering flames spewing out vulgarities and cursing God.

Dane didn't want to think about where he was, but he couldn't deny it—he was in hell, but he wasn't dead—or was he?

Walking along the edge of the burning embers, he noticed the fire did not consume the bodies. Then he saw some chained spirits. The ugly, vile creatures were quite tall, taller than humans. Who were they?

When the entities in the fire saw Dane, they cried out, "Save us from the wrath of God!"

Petrified, Dane ran aimlessly, but his surroundings never changed. What he saw only added to his terror. He came upon revulsive creatures with tentacles reaching out to grab him.

As he avoided the body snatchers, he noticed the bodies were males in the burning flames. They swayed in the inferno, seductively trying to lure him hither. Unintentionally, he locked eyes with one. The attraction was so strong he couldn't peel away. He felt trapped and defenseless as a seducing, evil spirit held on to him like glue.

Despite Dane's attempt to disengage, he couldn't. He felt his little strength, including his will to live, being sucked out of him. At the last second, Dane cried out, "Jesus!"

Immediately the trance broke, and Dane collapsed onto scampering giant roaches looking for food. With angelic help, he jumped to his feet. Overcome with dread of being sucked into the fire again, he shouted once more, "Jesus!"

———

The college student found himself standing beside his car at the exact spot where he had left it. He saw houses along the road—buildings that weren't there before, and streetlights lit the road. He leaned against his car and sobbed. "Thank you, Jesus. Forgive me."

For the first time, he realized that choosing a lifestyle forbidden in the Bible was like choosing death over life. Without repentance, his payment would be an earlier death than normal and eternal separation from God.

The attraction to a gay lifestyle over, Dane recognized it for what it was, a strong delusion. Perhaps he wasn't tempted by power, fame, or money, but sin enticed everybody, and the devil used this sin to blind him to God's truth.

Now he wanted to start over. He would read his Bible and find a church. First, he would retrieve his phone at his parent's house.

Dane unlocked his car and climbed in. To his amazement, the car started. "Thank you, Jesus," and he took off. Not only did he want to share with his parents that God had answered his challenge, but he also wanted to hear more about where his father came from—where men were boys and women were girls.[1]

17

THE LAST DANCE

Numbers 32:23 (NKJV)

... you have sinned against the LORD; and be sure your
   sin will find you out.

Christmas lights adorned the streets of Buckhead near downtown Atlanta. Colorful trimmings lit up Lenox Square, and a beautiful Christmas tree sent Good Tidings to all who passed by the iconic shopping center. Earl Ludwick enjoyed the crispness of the winter air—not too cold, but enough to make the trees barren until spring.

He turned into the Solar Roofing, Inc., parking lot for the annual Christmas party. Divorced, he didn't have anyone to accompany him, but his preeminent position in the solar world made him a sought-after "companion" for the evening. At least, that was his view of things.

Earl exited the car and took the elevator up to the top floor as soft Christmas music streamed on the intercom radio. When the door opened, the security guard waved him through. "Good evening, Mr. Ludwick."

The music must have put the executive in a festive mood. He smiled at the lowly guard. "Merry Christmas."

When Earl entered the decorated room, the party was in full swing. A warm reception greeted him, and after the perfunctory greetings, he strolled over to the food cart.

"Would you like some Christmas punch?" the server asked.

Earl nodded. "With rum."

Holding his drink, the man grabbed a table on the dance floor. He'd need two brews to unwind enough to dance, but he had lots of time. The party would become more lively in the wee hours.

His secretary joined him, giving him the eye. He smiled. Since he had already spent an evening with her, he was looking for the company's new hire. She was a knock-out blonde, and Earl knew with her wit and charisma, she would soon become a top saleswoman.

The executive had an uncanny ability to see talent before anyone else, and his knack for recognizing aptitudes in people had helped to propel the company to the top of the solar industry.

His secretary, Janet, prodded him. "You're looking for Rhonda, aren't you?"

Caught off-guard, he asked, "What are you, a mind reader?"

Janet laughed. "Why are you so surprised? I read your text messages on the computer app and pretend I'm you. You know that."

Earl took a swig from his drink. She saved him time by responding to all the messages from company peons. He forgot that made her privy to his personal life. "Well, let her know I'd love a dance if you see her."

Janet nodded, again giving him the eye. "I will if she comes," and she strolled away. Earl noticed how good she looked in high heels.

Another talent Earl had was his ability to pick up on nonverbal cues. He knew who was gay, who was straight, who the trouble-makers were, and who would betray him to take his position. He also knew that people would let down their guard after a few drinks. The gossip tantalized Earl. He liked knowing the forbidden knowledge.

People's secrets gave him power, and he had met with much success. Earl had spent the night with every woman in the company that interested him—except for one, Jenny Sables. She was not the best-looking girl he had ever laid eyes on, but everyone knew she was a Christian. Her life was, well, different. He had propositioned her once, and she turned him down. As if that wasn't enough to humble him, later, she gave him a tract about salvation.

He saw Jenny in the back of the room talking to another woman. He thought about walking over to say hi but didn't want to get into a long conversation in case Rhonda showed up. He needed to keep his options open. With over thirty people in the room, if he missed Rhonda, somebody else would catch her.

The night went on, and when Earl was on his third drink—he usually stopped at three so he could be sober enough to drive—and Rhonda hadn't appeared, he figured she wasn't coming. So he walked over to Jenny. The girl Jenny was talking to had left.

Earl sat in a chair beside her. He didn't know any gossip about

Jenny because she never gossiped. All he knew was that she was a Christian. "Merry Christmas."

Jenny smiled.

"Do you want to dance?" Earl asked.

"Sure," she said.

Surprised—he didn't think Christians danced—he took her hand, and they strolled to the dance floor. After dimming the lights, the band switched to some slow romantic music, and everyone on the floor cleared out of the way. Earl held Jenny in his arms, and they danced to two Christmas songs.

Was it the music that moved him? Or was there something about Jenny that was different? She was an excellent dancer and moved with such grace he imagined her floating in the air. Some girls were all over the place, but Jenny knew where to put her feet, arms, and body.

When the second dance ended, she released her hand from Earl's shoulder. "That's my last dance," she said, and returned to the table.

"What did she mean by that?" Earl mumbled. He followed her. "You're an amazing dancer."

Jenny smiled. "Thank you. I took ballet lessons as a child."

"Oh." Earl bit his lip. "I didn't think Christians danced."

Jenny laughed. "Maybe Baptists don't dance, but I dance. I dance for the glory of God."

"You dance..." Earl had no idea what she meant. He noticed she had a drink. No doubt she didn't add the rum, which was optional. Earl suddenly realized how little he knew about Christians. And all he knew about Jenny was that she wouldn't sleep with him.

"Excuse me," she said. "I'm going to get some more desserts."

Earl nodded. His eyes followed Jenny as she disappeared into the crowd. Then he noticed her drink sitting beside her empty plate. What if he spiked her drink? She would never know it. He thought about what it would be like to have her. He had never been denied— except by her. He remembered their dance, her breath on his cheeks, and the perfume she wore. He longed to make his desire come true. He may not have another perfect opportunity. No one would know.

Earl peered into the crowd to see if he could see her. Then he reached into his pocket to pull out the mischief. How much? His hands shook. He remembered her strange words, "This is my last dance."

Suppose he put too much in her drink. Were her words an omen that he would kill her? Rape was one thing, but murder was another. Of course, he had never raped anyone—or had he? He didn't want to remember. If he hadn't raped anyone, then why did he have this mischief in his pocket?

Earl felt himself getting dizzy. He didn't want to remember.

"You are a rapist," he heard a voice say in his head. "How many women have you raped?"

Earl's head spun. He wasn't a rapist. He had never hurt anyone. He had just made love to many women. Too many to count. Earl shook his head to clear his mind. He admitted, yes, he had date raped many women, but that was different. He made them feel good. He had no remorse about what he had done. He had never hurt anyone —or had he?

He shook his head. "No, I never hurt anyone." If he was going to spike Jenny's drink, he needed to do it quickly before she returned. His desire for her seeped into his lustful thoughts. He opened the mischief, but as he started to pour it into her drink, Rhonda plopped beside him. Rhonda, the one he had been waiting to see.

She smiled, and her eyes peered into his. "What's that in your hand?"

Startled, he dropped it on the floor. "Oh, it's just stuff for heartburn," he said, pretending it was his drink.

She picked it up and handed it to him.

"I don't want it now that it's been on the floor." He tossed it on the table.

"So, who's sitting here? I see a purse. I didn't mean to intrude."

"Oh, no, you aren't intruding. Jenny went to get some more desserts." He peered in that direction. "She's been gone awhile."

Suddenly the lights flickered on and off. The music stopped. Earl heard his phone ringing, and he put it up to his ear. "What?" he said. "You're talking so fast, I can't understand you."

Gasps and screams filled the room. People began to disperse in a panic.

Earl watched Rhonda grab her stuff and leave.

No matter how hard he tried, he couldn't understand his son's words. "Let me go outside. I can't understand anything you're saying," but the phone clicked as his son hung up.

Flustered, he stuck the phone in his back pocket. He needed to get out of the building. Where was Jenny? What about her purse? Should he leave it here? Maybe he should take her bag with him. If he didn't take it, somebody might steal it. Perhaps he might learn some things about her.

He grabbed it and headed to the exit. As he passed by the dessert cart, his eyes beheld the most startling thing he had ever seen. Jenny's clothes were on the carpet in a heap, as if she had disrobed. He looked around the room amid the chaos. Where did she go?

18

THE DRAGON

John 8:44 (NKJV)

"You are of your father the devil, and the desires of
your father you want to do. He was a murderer
from the beginning, and does not stand in the
truth, because there is no truth in him. When he
speaks a lie, he speaks from his own resources, for
he is a liar and the father of it."

The Dragon smacked his lips as he solidified plans. His self-appointed supremacy would usurp God's self-righteousness. "I will ascend above the heights of the clouds; I will be like the Highest."

As soon as God snatched away the Christians, the Dragon immediately dispatched his army to earth. "Cause as much chaos as possible," he fumed.

Many details remained to be determined before the seven-year Tribulation began. The confirmation of the treaty with Israel was the next major event on the timeline. Lucifer's thoughts transported him into the future. Could he defeat Jesus Christ in the battle of Armageddon? The Dragon's pride would not allow him to admit defeat.

In the event of Jesus' unlikely triumph, Lucifer would take as many rancid humans with him as possible. His abode was large enough to hold all the humans on the planet. Lucifer derided Jesus. "God's Son died on the cross like a commoner. How could he defeat me, the Prince of Darkness?"

His progeny, the Beast, and the False Prophet waited in the wings to take their seats of power. Midnight struck with the snatching away. Thousands of years separated the inciting event in the Garden of Eden when he, in the guise of a snake, deceived Eve. Most humans went to hell, but God wasn't willing to let anyone who believed in him perish. The last human to accept Jesus as his Savior took his good ole time. "What a waste—one measly human practically stopped time," the Dragon seethed..

His blasphemous tirade continued. "I hate humans. They get in the way of progress." But his time to shine would come soon enough.

Next up was the Ezekiel War. At least, that was Lucifer's assessment. Of course, the two witnesses would soon appear, and the 144,000 Jewish evangelists would be a problem. His warriors couldn't eliminate them. What a shame, but God drew the battle lines, another unfair advantage.

The Dragon lamented; if only he could be in more than one place at one time like God—another unfair advantage. He had to rely on his minions for updated reports about the most sensitive areas in the world—like Israel, Russia, Turkey, Iran, Iraq, Syria, Spain, France, England, Italy, Greece, and the northern coast of Africa. The United States was not part of the ten-nation confederacy so he wouldn't waste time with them. The King of Babylon would eventually control them as a vassal state.

He flipped on his secret source to see how events were unraveling worldwide. He had dispatched his minions to the King of Babylon and the ten little kings when the raptured happened, and the doomsday clock would start ticking when the Willful King signed the treaty with Israel.

The Dragon cursed the God of Heaven. He did not know when that seven years would start—if he had six months or six years. The longer the setup took, the more likely humans would read the Bible. He needed to devise a plan to destroy all the books about God, particularly any book that shared the Gospel. The sooner the midpoint of the Tribulation arrived, the better.

The Instrument of Deception fumed. "God does not play fair. How can I launch a counterattack when vital information is withheld!" But that didn't matter. His host of fallen angels, highly skilled in deception, would prevail. The World Economic Forum and other global organizations did their bidding exceptionally well.

Plus, to his advantage, no matter how little sense it made, people believed lies more quickly than they believed truth. Lucifer laughed. Humans were useless. First, they lose the ability to think. Once that happens, they no longer want to think. "And that works in my favor," Lucifer sneered.

Laziness, that's what it was. Lucifer quoted from the holy book. "Idle hands are a devil's workshop." However, people didn't read their Bible. People didn't read hardly anything—but give them unseemly words to tickle their ears and pornography to tempt their eyes—most chose that over the Bible, even if it cost them eternal damnation.

The Dragon remembered the guy who said if he accepted Jesus, he couldn't go to bed with that good-looking chic he had just met. "I'll think about it," he said. He did not know God would demand his soul that night.

Of course, some preferred mind-altering alchemy for pleasure, better known as witchcraft. "As old as time, those tricks," Satan quipped. Unredeemed human nature never changed. It just morphed into something more wicked.

Lucifer smirked. If he could deceive one-third of the angels to rebel against God, he'd have no problem deceiving the poor little earthlings left behind. And wait until the extraterrestrial arrives. The Vatican had their telescopes scouring the sky, anticipating his arrival.

The extraterrestrial's power would include lying wonders and magic, even bringing fire down from heaven. The Whore of Babylon would implement worshipping the earth goddess, and the Central Bank Digital Currency would centralize money worldwide into a one-world digital economy. With the mandatory mark of the beast, the King of Babylon's power would be so absolute that he would cause all, small and great, to worship him. When the Man of Sin suffered a mortal wound, the Dragon would possess him in a fake resurrection. He smiled, swooning at defeating the enemy.

Sheep among wolves—the Dragon loved the way that sounded. Lucifer knew his enemy very well. As one of the angels closest to God before the rebellion, he knew God better than any other created Elohim.

If he were God, he sure wouldn't have allowed the Apostle John to write the book of Revelation. John gave away almost all of Yeshua's secrets about the future. "Stupid strategy," Satan scoffed. However, most humans didn't bother to read the book anyway, claiming it was too hard to understand or they were just allegorical stories and nothing more.

However, Lucifer had to give God credit for one thing. The Dragon was the most beautiful being he created. Never mind if people called him a fallen angel. They didn't know the truth about God.

Satan would prove that he was more worthy than God. He'd start by killing all the humans—all of them. Even though he failed to kill Jesus when he was on the earth the first time, he would have another opportunity at the battle of Armageddon.

But getting back to the sheep, the Dragon's forces were like ravenous wolves, hungry for humans, destined to annihilate most of the earthlings God pitied. His minions would destroy God's sheep through famine, poison, pestilence, and nuclear war. Soon the four angels chained in the Euphrates River would be released, and they would spearhead the death of one-third of humanity at the behest of two hundred million super-killers.

Smelling blood, the Dragon licked his lips. The stench was as sweet as bitter.

19

COLLAR OF LISIANTHUS

Matthew 19:14 (NKJV)

But Jesus said, "Let the little children come to Me, and do not forbid them; for of such is the kingdom of heaven."

White Dog heard a knock on his door.

He peered out the window and saw Alvis, the old bear from Lisianthus, standing on his porch.

"Why would Alvis visit me unless something big has happened in Lisianthus?" he muttered.

When White Dog opened the door, the bear dispensed with the pleasantries and immediately conveyed the urgency of his visit.

"White Dog, we need your help. Our great leader has died, and we have two lions vying to take over the kingship. However, the animals are undecided about who should be king, and the lions have threatened to kill each other. If that were to happen, Lisianthus would be weakened and more susceptible to attack. We know the God of the heavens always talks to you. The animals sent me to seek your advice."

White Dog invited Alvis into his tiny abode and pointed to a solid place he could sit. White Dog only weighed a fraction of Alvis, and his furniture was not designed for a giant bear.

"Tell me about the two contenders to the throne," White Dog said.

Alvis replied, "One of the lions is handsome with a beautiful flowing mane, and words flow easily from his lips. He roars like a lion, but—I don't think he's wise like our old leader."

"What about the second contender?" White Dog asked.

Alvis shuddered. "The second contender is full of pride. He's arrogant and deceives most of the animals."

Resignation filled Alvis' brown face. "I don't think either contender would make a good ruler. How do you choose between two bad contenders? What should we do?"

"What do the animals of Lisianthus say?" White Dog asked.

Alvis replied. "Some say let the two lions fight to the death for supremacy, but most of the animals of Lisianthus don't want that. They believe the fight would hurt the country and make it vulnerable."

"What do you want from me?" White Dog asked.

Alvis stood, and his big brown body towered over White Dog. "We want you to come to Lisianthus and choose our next king."

White Dog thought about Alvis' proposal. Finally, he replied. "Under one condition."

"What's that?" Alvis asked.

"Both sides must agree to my decision."

Alvis nodded. "I already told the animals if I came to ask for your help, they would have to accept your advice. I promise you, they will. They will keep their word."

"First, let me seek God's will. Let's pray for a couple of days," White Dog said.

Two days later, White Dog and Alvis returned to Lisianthus. The animals set up a great reception to greet them, and anticipation ran high that a resolution would soon come to pass.

"I must speak to the contending lions," White Dog said. "Can you bring them to me?"

————

White Dog examined the two lions vying for the throne for several hours.

At last, White Dog spoke, "I have come to a decision."

The animals set a time to hear his proclamation.

At the appointed time, thousands of animals popped out of the nooks and crannies of Lisianthus to hear White Dog's verdict.

White Dog stood on a tall rock so that everyone could hear him. After waiting for the noise to die, he addressed the anxious crowd. "Neither of the contenders is qualified. Neither of them is worthy of being your king. Smooth words or a pompous spirit is not God's way."

At this proclamation, rumblings filled the crowd.

"However," White Dog said. "I have more to say. Are there any other lions in Lisianthus that are of age?"

Several replied, "Only one, but he is lame."

"Bring him to me," White Dog demanded.

Alvis knew where he lived and went to get him. A short time later, he brought the lame lion to the circle of succession, where the other two contenders waited beneath the tall rock for White Dog to speak.

White Dog beseeched God, "Which of these lions should be the next king of Lisianthus?"

As White Dog waited for God to speak, he closed his eyes and stood at attention. After several minutes, he faced the crowd to announce what the God of the heavens had declared.

Everyone became silent as White Dog spoke. "The next king is the lame lion, and his new name is Sure Foot."

Laughter arose from the crowd. The two contenders stared at White Dog.

"Is this a joke?" the arrogant one asked.

White Dog ignored his question and walked over to the lame lion. The soon-to-be-appointed king stood stoic as White Dog put the Lisianthus flowers around his neck. The lion who wore the collar was recognized as the king of Lisianthus. The flowers signified the rebirth of the kingdom under the new king.

White Dog said, "Sure Foot knows he can't lead without the help of God. He knows the battle belongs to the Lord. And he will discover the more he trusts God, the stronger his legs will become. Soon his hind legs will be stronger than all the other animals of Lisianthus and even its enemies."

A mixed reaction stirred among the crowd. Some thought White Dog was wise. Others weren't sure. However, because of the animals' agreement with White Dog, they accepted Sure Foot as their new leader.

After the coronation, White Dog returned to his home. He heard that an orderly succession took place, and as recorded in the annals of Lisianthus, the country was safe from warring nations for the next twenty years. With humility, Sure Foot governed, and with strength, he ruled Lisianthus all the days he was king.

———

As a reader, you might be wondering why this short story is included in *The Night Cometh*. Let me share my heart. Look around. Evaluate the world. This would be a different place if God's people would repent, pray, and call on the Lord. If Christian leaders would intercede and cry out to Jesus Christ, we could have revival. If people would obey the law, lawlessness would not abound. The spirit of the Antichrist can only be fought with God's weapons, and they are not carnal. They are spiritual.

———

20

TWINKLING

The last story in this collection, "The Twinkling," is part memoir and part sanctified imagination. I did not want to end *The Night Cometh* focused on the horrors in these short stories.

The Biblical story is about God providing a way for humans to be part of his family. He wanted an earthly family like he had a heavenly family—forever. That means for all eternity.

Salvation is a prayer away. Call on the Lord. Repent. Grab a Bible, and start reading. Be "born again."

———

As I gently stroked my cat, I leaned over and kissed her. "I love you, Twila." My gray thirteen-year-old feline lay on a soft blanket. For five months, I had kept her going with a good quality of life, but her weakened heart was beating its last. Her days to live were perhaps only hours. She purred unceasingly as she rested. Her joy in living was that I was with her.

In her eyes, I was like our heavenly Father. She did not want to let go because she did not want to leave me. I prayed that God would take her gently in the night, and before the light of dawn, she was with her Maker.

While sin ravages the soul, God put us here to occupy until his blessed return. We're to spread his love to the beasts, the fowl, and, as far as possible, to our family, neighbors, and friends. Even those prickly people who worm their way into our lives.

Because our pets do not live very long, the death of one reminds us of how temporary this world is. While we grieve when they die, sometimes unexpectedly, we do not grieve like those without hope. Nevertheless, the sting of death hurts.

That sting reminds me that someday my body will give out, too, or an untoward event will take me, or God will rapture his church. The Bible says it is appointed unto man once to die, and after that, the judgment (Hebrews 9:27).

I find comfort in knowing that what we see isn't all there is to this sometimes meaningless existence. Perhaps the unseen world is more real. Because God is a God of comfort, his unceasing care allows us to comfort others with his love, even our precious pets. As Twila made her journey to eternity, I thanked God for letting me suffer with her.

As Christians, when we suffer, we enter into God's protective covering. Perhaps it doesn't make sense, but we long for God in our suffering. We behold his majesty and want to be like him when we embrace his mercy.

Someday, I will see Twila again, along with all the other dogs and cats that have blessed me since I was a child.

For the creation was subjected to futility, not willingly, but because of him who subjected *it* in hope; because the creation itself also will be delivered from the bondage of corruption into the glorious liberty of the children of God. For we know that the whole creation groans and labors with birth pangs together until now. Not only that, but we also who have the first fruits of the Spirit, even we ourselves groan within ourselves, eagerly waiting for the adoption, the redemption of our body. For we were saved in this hope, but hope that is seen is not hope; for why does one still hope for what he sees? But if we hope for what we do not see, *we eagerly wait for it with perseverance.* [emphasis mine] Romans 8:20-25 (NKJV)

When we're born again, we're no longer sons and daughters of Adam but sons and daughters of the Most High God. Rebirth in the Spirit is only the first step. That allows us to be God's ambassadors here on earth and to share the Good News of Jesus' soon return.

Someday, Jesus will return in what Scripture refers to as the Blessed Hope. After the rapture, we'll be clothed in new bodies and born again with bodies that will allow us to inhabit heaven.

---

1 Corinthians 15:51-52 (NKJV)

Behold, I tell you a mystery: We shall not all sleep, but
    we shall all be changed—in a moment, in the
    twinkling of an eye, at the last trumpet. For the
    trumpet will sound, and the dead will be raised
    incorruptible, and we shall be changed.

A loud shout awakens me from my slumber, followed by another voice echoing the exact words as the first. The voices rumble with authority I dare not ignore. "Come up here!"

Long blasts from a trumpet herald the words, and as my eyes and ears alert me to something spectacular, I ask, "Is this another rapture dream, or is this for real?"

I feel the Spirit snatch me from my bed, and as I effortlessly leave the house through the roof, a bright light twinkles from the sky. Upon leaving the first heaven and arriving in the second, I see my Lord and Savior in the clouds.

————

In the twinkling of an eye, my body changed. The day for which I had longed was here. Year after year, even as others asked, "Where is the promise of his coming?" I waited for my Savior's return.

In season and out of season, I prayed. With all my strength, I anticipated this day. I longed to hear my Savior call my name from the grave or at the rapture. I never doubted the Blessed Hope of his appearing before the Tribulation.

————

As I soar through the celestial realm, the earth disappears behind me, and my new body, not limited by time and space, can travel "where no man has gone before." Now that I'm outside the confines of everyday human activity, death is swallowed up in victory.

I gaze into the star-filled heavens as the celestial world reveals its hidden treasures. I could only comprehend four dimensions of the universe in my earthly body. Now, because of God's revelation, I can witness much more. I see beyond length, width, depth, and time, and while soaring like a bird, I hear the stars exalting my Lord and Savior.

Indeed, I discover my new body is far superior to my old one. My heightened perceptions reveal the limitations of my former human "hardware." My hearing is so acute I imagine I could hear a pin drop light-years away. How did Jesus Christ humble himself to such a low estate?

I no longer need glasses. I laugh as they are on the vanity beside my bed. My corruptible body has been made perfect. No more follow-ups for breast cancer. No more root canals. No more Covid or pestilences, or wars or rumors of wars.

When I was little, I watched my great-grandfather remove his fake teeth. I wondered if someday I would have removable teeth, too. I imagined I'd probably lose them or swallow them. I wondered what it would be like not to have any teeth at all. That will never happen now.

As I take it all in, I remind myself nothing is fake in heaven. Everything is real, and that's just the beginning. No more sitting in city traffic, preparing for unpredictable hurricanes, or filing tax returns. No more lawsuits or empty grocery store shelves or saying goodbye.

As I see the earth spinning among the stars, the Blessed Hope of the rapture is opening graves worldwide. Millions of transformed souls are on the long-awaited trip to heaven with me.

Yeshua Hamashiach—known by some as the carpenter from Galilee and others by names not worthy of mention—is escorting us beneath his wings, taking his followers to a heavenly abode.

Jesus has been preparing the dwelling place of his bride for two thousand years. I can't wait to reach our destination. My attachment to my former home is already broken as I anticipate my eternal home in heaven.

My focus heavenward, I smile, remembering conversations with Christians who denied the rapture or believed it would happen much later, perhaps not until the end of the Great Tribulation.

I always asked those of that mindset, "Is Jesus going to let his bride be killed, maimed, or raped?"

When Jesus opens the first seal, that's an important milestone.

To be on the crimson-stained earth after the opening of the second seal will be horrid for those left behind.

Clothed in garments of pure white, I am a beautiful bride. No suffering shall ever touch me again. I will not feel the horrid heat of the sun, see locusts from the bottomless pit, or witness a sword coming down on my neck. Never again will the Bible-believing church face an attack from the demonic realm. The unannounced appearance in the clouds of Jesus Christ is the Blessed Hope.

In Matthew 24:43 (ESV), Jesus said, "...if the master of the house had known in what part of the night the thief was coming, he would have stayed awake and would not have let his house be broken into."

God never shared the day or hour of Jesus' return. I took his Word to heart and believed, with child-like faith, that Jesus could come at any time. Now, clothed in my new body, I am his bride.

I praise God, who knew me from the world's foundations, breathed life into me, and smiled over that cluster of cells as they took shape inside my mother's womb. Even in my sin, he loved me. He knew my flaws and propensity to sin and assigned angels to take charge over me and protect me.

All the wonders of God's majesty are becoming more evident. Among the stars, the whole universe speaks of God's glory. If only I had known how much God loved me as an earthling. If only I had known how much the Holy Spirit protected me. If only I had known how much the angels intervened on my behalf.

I see now the power that was at my disposal. I could have thwarted the demonic forces at any time by calling on Jesus. Those vile creatures sought to prevent my entrance into God's eternal kingdom, but demons flee in cowardly retreat at the mention of Jesus.

Praise God the former things have passed away. As I approach the third heaven, I see an open door. All around me are heaven-bound travelers. I search for my earthly family and loved ones. The Savior is standing at the door inviting his bride to enter. Millions of redeemed souls, saved by Jesus' atoning work on the cross, enter.

As I near the heavenly gates, the angels sing my name. Even I, so lowly and insignificant, because of Jesus, am counted worthy.

———

In the beginning, Lucifer contaminated God's earthly abode in the Garden of Eden. Since that dreadful day, earthlings have been separated from God. I used to imagine what the Garden of Eden was like—to commune with Jesus in a perfect garden filled with animals that he spoke into existence. To have such intimacy with the Lord must have been surreal.

God reveals his glory in his creation. Regal animals, delicate flowers, towering trees, thunderous waters, flittering butterflies, and singing birds speak of his majesty. To be able to talk to the animals, who had no fear of humans, to receive and give perfect love—oh, what a loss.

I thought the Garden of Eden was gone forever. As I grew in the knowledge of God, God revealed to me my flawed understanding. Paradise is not lost. The reversal has begun that will return us to the Garden of Eden.

As I await entrance into the presence of God, millions of other redeemed citizens surround me. Songs of praise fill the heavens, from the nearest point of the universe to the farthermost. I gaze ahead with great anticipation.

My turn to enter arrives. As I pass through the eternal gates, the scene is too spectacular to describe. Once inside, I kneel on the flowery ground and praise my Savior. Never again will I be separated from him.

Soon, Jesus, as King of Kings, will take his rightful place in the heavenly temple to judge his church. My heart pounds. Will I be deemed worthy?

Following the rewards ceremony, Jesus will marry his bride, and we'll enjoy the heavenly mansion he has prepared for us for the next seven years. When the allotted days on earth have passed, known as the Great Tribulation, Jesus will return to earth as King of Kings and set up his Kingship in Jerusalem.

As I contemplate the unfolding of events, I see millions of joyful reunions. My loved ones have discovered me—my daughters, my mother, my father, my grandparents, my brother, my sister, my friends, and my acquaintances. Too many to count. We're celebrating with all the redeemed saints since Pentecost.

No longer in bondage to sin, our redemption as the sons and daughters of God has set the animals free. I see my beloved pets.

While heaven is celebrating, the woes on earth are only beginning. The first seal awaits opening. The white horse will go out to conquer, followed by the red horse of war. The third horse will bring famine, and the last horse will bring death.

Seven long years of sorrow will follow after the Antichrist confirms the covenant. While we're receiving rewards and getting married, the left-behind earth-dwellers are about to endure the worst suffering imaginable.

My focus returns to the present. Tears fill my eyes. Some people I only know from afar. Some redeemed saints ministered to me through books, sermons, bible studies, or perhaps spoke a word of encouragement. Too many to count; eternity will allow me to meet each one again and thank them.

I hug my mom and dad. I hug my children. I hug my grandparents. I hug my friends. I hug strangers. I hug anyone and everyone within arm's reach. We are brothers and sisters in Christ.

And while all these reunions are beyond measure, the one I long to hug is my Lord and Savior. Even now, I sense his presence beside me. As I touch my new body, I remember I will never again experience sorrow. My "hardware" is no longer of flesh and blood. Humbled, I remember I'm here only because Jesus died for me.

As I think about the judgment seat for believers, God brings to remembrance the martyrs. A crown is set aside for them. In losing their lives for Christ, they will receive the crown of life.

I remember the missionaries who traveled thousands of miles

over two thousand years to share the Good News. I think about the missionaries to the unborn. I recall books written by scholars, pastors, and laypeople. And what about the linguists who spent lifetimes translating the Bible into native languages so people could read God's Word in their own tongue? The soul winner's crown awaits them.

I think about the incorruptible crown earned by those who fought the good fight and ran the race with perseverance—believers who never gave up, gave in, or compromised. The victory crown awaits them.

As I remember all these things, God reminds me that some of the redeemed may not earn a crown or receive anything. Too many will see the rewards they lost and the crowns they forfeited because they failed to finish well.

Rewards or no rewards, the bema seat is not about salvation. God's grace saves even those who have no fruit or good works. Jesus' gift of salvation is the same for all—those who accepted Jesus into their hearts on their deathbeds and those who served Jesus their entire lives.

As I ponder these thoughts, I see a multitude gathering. The heavenly temple is open, and angelic beings encircle the throne. Seated on the throne is Jesus. A rainbow layered with green and red gemstones surrounds him.

As I witness my risen Savior as King, his holiness strikes me. His hair is white like wool, as white as snow, and his eyes are like a flame of fire.

Every creature shouts in unison, "Worthy is the Lamb who was slain to receive power and riches and wisdom, and strength and honor and glory and blessing!" (Rev 5:12 NKJV) .

I bow in worship.

Around the throne twenty-four elders clothed in white raiment are wearing golden crowns. Despite the multitude present, I am aware that many souls are absent. Those who rejected Christ during the age of grace will face judgment after the millennium. The Old

Testament believers and those who accepted Jesus during the Tribulation will be resurrected when Jesus returns.

A holy quietness fills the temple. All eyes focus on the unfolding scene. In front of King Yeshua stands a redeemed human. Soon, I will stand before Jesus, as will all redeemed saints.

I do not know the man's identity. Is he one of the apostles—Peter, James, John, or Paul? Is he a great Christian leader? The Holy Spirit admonishes me to watch.

Jesus places a crown on the man's head, and his words reverberate across the heavens in a voice that sounds like many waters. "At my crucifixion, you asked, 'Remember me when you come into your kingdom,' and I promised you, as I hung on the cross, 'Today, thou shalt be with me in paradise.'"

Gasps erupt as millions, perhaps billions, praise King Yeshua. Among the redeemed in heaven are former murderers, fornicators, and idolators. Some died proclaiming with their last breath, "I believe in Jesus," remembering the thief who died alongside Jesus.

A great chorus of singing erupts, and I join them singing at the top of my lungs, "How great thou art..."

I have much to learn about greatness. Perhaps many I once considered to be great will not be so. I have already seen a few souls I did not expect to be here. And maybe, some thought the same about me. As Jesus foretold two thousand years ago, the first will be last, and the last will be first.

As my moment approaches to stand before King Yeshua, I hope to receive the crown of righteousness given to those who long for his appearing. I marvel, treasuring all these thoughts, and I remember the words to a favorite hymn, "Amazing love, how can it be, that thou, my God, should die for me?" [1]

After these events, Jesus will return to earth as King of Kings. The bride of Jesus will be with him riding on white horses, and after disposing of his enemies, King Yeshua will set up his throne in Jerusalem.

But for now, at this moment, in one solemn voice, the angels and redeemed saints proclaim, "Alleluia! Salvation and glory and honor and power belong to the Lord our God" Rev 19:1 (NKJV).

NOTES

CHAPTER 3

1. Reedsyprompts. Submitted to Contest #157 in response to: Write about two characters who both want what the other has, without knowing the feeling is mutual. http://blog.reedsy.com/creative-writing-prompts/author/lorilyn-roberts/

CHAPTER 4

1. 2021 Florida Christian Writers' Conference second-place winner for short story/flash fiction.

CHAPTER 5

1. Reedsyprompts. Submitted to Contest #160 in response to: Write about someone seeking an oasis in a desert—whether literally, or figuratively. http://blog.reedsy.com/creative-writing-prompts/author/lorilyn-roberts/

CHAPTER 6

1. Reedsyprompts. Submitted to Contest #165 in response to: Write a story that includes the phrase "This is all my fault." http://blog.reedsy.com/creative-writing-prompts/author/lorilyn-roberts/

CHAPTER 7

1. Reedsyprompts. Submitted to Contest #158 in response to: Write a story that includes someone saying, "It's not fair." http://blog.reedsy.com/creative-writing-prompts/author/lorilyn-roberts/

CHAPTER 10

1. Reedsyprompts. Submitted to Contest #161 in response to: Write a story where someone finds comfort in an unexpected event, place, or person. http://blog.reedsy.com/creative-writing-prompts/author/lorilyn-roberts/

CHAPTER 12

1. Reedsyprompts. Submitted to Contest #159 in response to: Set your story in a world where the currency isn't money — or at least not money as we understand it. http://blog.reedsy.com/creative-writing-prompts/author/lorilyn-roberts/

CHAPTER 13

1. Reedsyprompts. Submitted to Contest #162 in response to: Write a story where a character's life completely changes over the course of a meal. http://blog.reedsy.com/creative-writing-prompts/author/lorilyn-roberts/

CHAPTER 14

1. Reedsyprompts. Submitted to Contest #156 in response to: Write about false news coverage of an important event. http://blog.reedsy.com/creative-writing-prompts/author/lorilyn-roberts/

CHAPTER 15

1. Roberts, Lorilyn. "Chapter 67." *Seventh Dimension - The Howling: A Young Adult Fantasy, Book 6,* edited by Lisa Lickel, 288-291. Gainesville, FL: Rear Guard Publishing, Inc., 2019.

CHAPTER 16

1. Reedsyprompts. Submitted to Contest #164 in response to: Start your story with a character saying "Where I come from..." http://blog.reedsy.com/creative-writing-prompts/author/lorilyn-roberts/

CHAPTER 20

1. *Amazing Love* or *And Can It Be That I Should Gain,* written by Charles Wesley. 1738.

ABOUT THE AUTHOR

Lorilyn Roberts is the author of fourteen books, including the award-winning *YA Seventh Dimension Series* and memoirs *Children of Dreams* and *Tails and Purrs for the Heart and Soul*. After scuba diving around the world and earning her college degree studying abroad, she settled into single motherhood, adopting two daughters from Nepal and Vietnam. She later earned a Master of Arts in Creative Writing and is president of the Gainesville, Florida, Chapter of Word Weavers International. Lorilyn has rescued many orphaned dogs and cats, and when she isn't writing books, she provides broadcast captioning for television. In her spare time, Lorilyn is a ham radio operator and CW/Morse Code enthusiast. KO4LBS.

ALSO BY LORILYN ROBERTS

LorilynRoberts.com

Children of Dreams

As an Audiobook

Tails and Purrs for the Heart and Soul

As an Audiobook

———

Look for the hidden word "good" on every page.

The Donkey and the King: A Story of Redemption

"Wonderful story with positive Christian values. Loved the illustrations. It's a hit with my kids!"

—"Goodreads" reader

Young readers become world leaders.

<u>Book Love</u>

"Book Love is beautiful inside and out. Roberts uses a child to teach children the love of books and it works beautifully. This book is a must for elementary classrooms and libraries. I highly recommend Book Love by Lorilyn Roberts if you have a child wanting to learn to read."

—Joy Hannabass, Readers' Favorite Reviewer

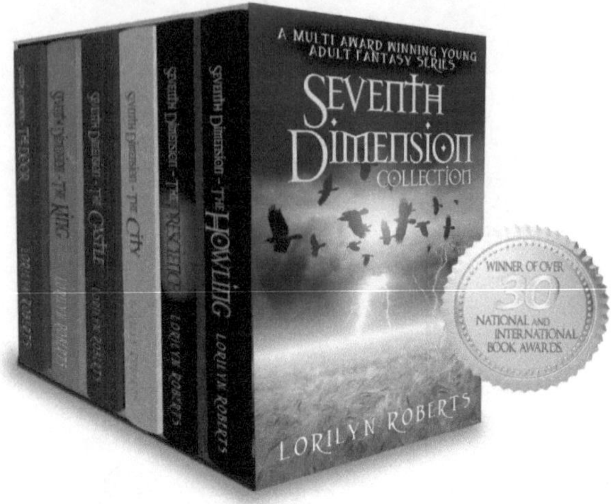

LorilynRoberts.com

Seventh Dimension - The Door, Book 1

As an Audiobook

Seventh Dimension - The King, Book 2

As an Audiobook

Seventh Dimension - The Castle, Book 3

As an Audiobook

Seventh Dimension - The City, Book 4

As an Audiobook

Seventh Dimension - The Prescience, Book 5

As an Audiobook

Seventh Dimension - The Howling, Book 6

As an Audiobook

———

LorilynRoberts.com

Food for Thought Cookbook

Seventh Dimension Devotional Series: Am I Okay,God?